AGE OF FIRE

FATED SERIES BOOK THREE

MARIAH STONE

Stone Publishing

ALSO BY MARIAH STONE

Mariah's Time travel Romance Series

- Called by a Highlander
- Called by a Viking
- Called by a Pirate
- Fated

Mariah's Regency Romance Series

- Dukes and Secrets

View all of Mariah's Books in Reading Order

Scan the QR code for the complete list of Mariah's ebooks, paperbacks, and audiobooks in reading order.

Some say the world will end in fire,
    Some say in ice.
    From what I've tasted of desire
    I hold with those who favor fire.
    But if it had to perish twice,
    I think I know enough of hate
    To say that for destruction ice
    Is also great
    And would suffice.

—Robert Frost

ONE

Holding Ella's hand, Channing walked through a white blizzard. It felt like they were the only people left in the universe.

Dark shapes of triple-deckers grayed on both sides of the street, but there were no lights in the windows. No music played, no neighbors quarrelled, and no dogs barked. A single streetlight flickered through the curtain of swirling snow.

Only a few weeks ago, Channing had invited himself to a shepherd's pie dinner at the O'Connor family's home. His chest had ached then, as he thought of what he had missed. This was a street where neighbors were friendly, children grew up together, and you couldn't take a step without someone knowing. This was a street where people were wary of strangers and held tightly to each other. Like the Viking world he'd just left behind.

Like his own family.

Now, it looked like Ragnarök was not just happening but had already ended. And this was afterwards.

Where had Dorchester Street gone? It had vanished with the rest of the world. Nothing would ever be the same.

And he was still from nowhere and had no home but this woman walking next to him. The woman who made his blood sizzle. The woman who brought the warmth of an open hearth right into the emptiness in his chest.

"Power must be out," Ella said, raising her voice over the howling wind.

He knew what she was worried about. His family was in the Viking Age. Hers was here...but were they okay? He wished he could ease her worry, shield her from everything. Wrap her in a protective cocoon.

He would die for her if he had to.

But was he ready to die for the world?

"We need to hurry, sweetheart," said Channing. "The storm is getting worse."

They sped up.

They had gotten a lift from the Port of Boston, and the driver had let them out a few blocks away. The street was impassable except on foot.

When they had left the port, with a sinking, cold desperation, Channing had realized the roads were almost carless. They'd walked south along Summer Street, where a few cars passed but never stopped. Most of the cars still running were electric. With the storms interfering with supply lines, the gas shortage was palpable.

Given their odd Viking clothes, Channing wasn't surprised no one would stop no matter how much they waved their arms. They carried no modern money, no credit cards, and no IDs. Their only possession in the world was the Viking travel backpack on Channing's back.

When they'd reached Dorchester Street, a driver had finally stopped. He'd agreed to give them a lift without payment, mumbling something about helping the homeless. About how the end of the world would reveal who we really are.

As they'd driven through South Boston, the car barely fit through the narrow streets. Ragnarök had made snowdrifts out of the parked cars. Rows of triple-deckers had flashed by, dark and lifeless. Bay windows and entrance doors of several were smashed. No children played in the streets. No dogs barked. No birds sang. The few gas stations they passed stood empty, prices for gas having increased tenfold. The driver told them power was out at least once a day now.

How was this better than the Viking Age? They had left his wounded father in the ninth century... Would his mother be able to save him from the gunshot wound? Would they defeat King Harald and his warriors, take back the singed mead hall, and get Hakon back on his feet?

Thoughts of his family were like knives slicing through the scabs of a wound that had never fully healed. Ella's hand in his soothed him like a cool balm. He'd lost his family, but she would find hers, and that was worth everything. Because her joy, her happiness was all he cared about.

"Do you even recognize any of the houses?" he asked, blinking fat, weightless snowflakes away.

"I think so," Ella said as she held back the edge of her white fur hood to look to her left. "Main thing is that I don't walk right past my house."

Snow was everywhere, in his eyes and on his neck, and in his nose. Wind stole his breath as it threw harsh gusts into his face.

Despite the snow and the silence, the thing that most concerned him was that they'd landed in a time where his port had been taken over by the Mafia, which told him two things. Number one, the police were weak enough to have let that happened. Number two, drugs would now flow freely into the city. Those shipments that made it through the storms, which would be even worse in the open seas, anyway.

Which meant there'd be more crime. The police would be helpless, if they weren't already.

Brothers killing brothers.

Fathers and sons' kinship bonds collapse.

More deaths.

Ragnarök was winning.

For a split second, he remembered the unforgiving, icy cold feel of the wooden stump pressed against his cheek. The sharp edge of the executioner's ax was about to fall.

That would have been it. At any moment, he'd have gone into the great unknown. Would it be Valhalla or something else?

And in those last moments, his life hadn't flashed before his eyes. He hadn't thought of what he should have done differently, of how to fight the two Vikings holding him down.

He'd seen one face in his mind's eye. Icy blue eyes under long, dark blond eyelashes. Her white teeth flashing as her pink lips curved up in a smile. How truly beautiful she was, and how lucky he'd been to have had her in his life, by his side.

And he'd wanted more. More time with her. More handholding. More kisses. More sex.

More everything.

He'd searched the white space infested by the enemies that had surrounded him in the circle. He wanted to be looking at her in his last moment.

There he'd been, trapped between love and death, the moment stretching like an eternity.

Submitting to what someone else thought was his destiny went against his nature. But a small part of him knew he should have just accepted his fate then. King Harald wanted to save the world by relieving it of Channing.

That would have been better for everyone.

Only, Ella hadn't let him.

One moment, Channing had seen her, trapped in the arms of King Harald. The next, she wasn't there. Someone had touched him, and he'd been sucked into a dark nothingness. And then he'd opened his eyes in the Port of Boston.

And he was alive. But should he be?

"There." She tugged him to her left, towards a bright orange and green spot behind the curtain of snow—a building.

The stairs of the front porch were a snowdrift, and they dug their shoes into the snow so as not to slip and fall. The windows were dark. Not surprisingly, the bell didn't work. Ella banged on the front door. No one answered.

"There are emergency generators in my building." Channing stepped up next to her and pounded on the door with his fist. "We're taking them to my apartment."

His apartment, at the top of the fifty-five-floor Infinity Tower, high above the Boston chaos, would be a fortress. No one would break in, and it would stay warm and there'd be light as long as the emergency generators worked. And they were geared for situations like this—that had been one of his requirements when he'd had the tower built.

The violent, rough Viking Age with its wooden longhouses, thatched roofs, and central hearths were one extreme. A cold, creaking triple-decker with no power was another.

"The port is not yours anymore," Ella mumbled. "Who's to say your apartment is?"

A THICK, cold silence followed her question. Channing must be contemplating the possibility of having lost both his business and his home. Maybe she shouldn't have brought it up.

In the quiet, she strained her ears, trying to catch a shuffle of feet from behind the front door, a click of the dead bolt being unlatched.

When steps sounded in the foyer, the world gained color. It must be Gloria. The steps were too heavy for Ted, and Dad was in a wheelchair. The peephole darkened for a moment, then nothing. On the tiny, convex circle of glass, Ella watched the two compacted and curved figures in Viking fur cloaks, covered in snow, trails of steam rushing out of their mouths.

"It's me!" she called.

The door flew open, and an ashen-faced Gloria stood in the frame. Two sweaters hugged her plump, short body. Her brown hair was messy, so unlike her, as though she hadn't brushed it for days. She wore winter boots and a beanie. Condensation pumped out of her mouth in small, erratic clouds.

Gloria gave out a high-pitched "Oh!" and hung on Ella's neck, her back shaking as she sobbed. Ella returned her hug and Gloria felt smaller, more delicate under Ella's palms, fragile like a doll.

And for the first time in her life the words *I'm back, Mom* were born in her throat.

She buried them deep down like she buried her face in Gloria's sweater, the wool scratchy against her cheek. She inhaled the familiar scent of old wood and a whiff of fried onions and garlic. A few moments later, Gloria backed into the dark hall of the triple-decker, wiping her eyes with the backs of her hands. "Come in, come in! Christ on a bike, you're back!"

Ella stepped into the semidark hallway that felt like a tunnel between worlds. Giant swirls of snow blew in after Channing as he followed her. Gloria shut the entrance door behind him, plunging them all into darkness. The scents of a home surrounded her—the chemical smell of cleaning products, the honey-like fragrance of old wood, and the distant scent of a kitchen.

Ella walked briskly towards the gray daylight shining through the apartment door.

She would see her dad and her brother in a moment. Anticipation burned her, the need, the longing for loved ones was like a strong wind pushing her forward.

"Dad!" Ella called. "Ted!"

Inside the apartment, two shadows appeared from the daylight of the living room. Her father, in the wheelchair, and her brother, Ted, a boy of twelve with Down's syndrome. Ella sank to her knees, hugging Ted first. Bryan caught her hand between his large palms, his skin dry and warm. Ted's eyes were teary, his lips trembling as Ella mumbled she was back, that she was okay, that she'd never leave him again.

As Gloria stepped into the apartment next to Channing and closed the door behind her, Ted grinned, his big eyes wide as he stared at him.

"Did you come with a big boat?" Ted asked him.

Channing grinned back. "Not this time, Ted."

"Hi, Dad." Ella hugged her father, and he wrapped his arm around her neck and patted the back of her fur cloak.

Bryan's lips tightened into a firm line as he looked at Channing.

"Thank you for bringing her back to me," he said.

Ella had expected a scowl, some reproach for being the reason his daughter had disappeared in time.

Not a thank-you.

"I didn't," Channing said. "It was all her."

Ella straightened up. Relief felt like a tiny sun glowing in her stomach. "Are you guys okay? Dad, have you started the cancer treatments?"

Bryan's face darkened. "We're fine. Come in, both of you. Tell me everything. I'll call Ricardo and you can thank him for getting Hakonson here out of jail."

The house was cold, and Channing suggested they go to his apartment, but Bryan told him the power would be back on soon.

While Bryan called Ricardo, Gloria brought Ella and Channing two glasses of cold water. It tasted chemical and artificial after the clean mountain water in the Viking Age, and, surprising herself, Ella longed for the warmth of a central hearth, the scent of woodsmoke, and Channing's family, fierce and loyal and loving. It would be wonderful to have both families together.

But that was impossible.

When her dad, Gloria, and Ted were all present, Ella began telling the story. She kept the most brutal details as general as possible given that her brother was listening. Soon, Ted seemed to lose interest. He asked Gloria to turn on the TV, but when she said the TV didn't work, he asked for his Rolf comic books.

Rolf was a superhero with an ability to throw lightning bolts and an ax that could cut anything. He was probably based on myths about Thor, and Ella wondered distantly how much there was about Ragnarök and about the Norns and the gods in the comic books.

In the middle of her story, a distant banging came from the front door.

Gloria went to open the door and returned accompanied by a wild-eyed, panting Ricardo.

<h1 style="text-align:center">TWO</h1>

As Ricardo scooped Ella into his embrace, a burning worm of jealousy turned in Channing's gut.

People were often misled by Ricardo's short, stocky stature and his goofy mannerisms, how he usually held back. But beneath the harmless exterior, Detective Ricardo Sanchez was a man of steel with a quick mind and a sharpshooter's eye.

And a beating heart that loved Channing's woman.

"*Chica*, where the hell have you been?" Ricardo murmured, his face buried in Ella's hair.

Channing's fist clenched. He shouldn't be feeling this way. Ella and Ricardo had been friends and partners in the police force for years.

Ella was Channing's. She loved him. She was committed to him. It was in his arms that she let her defenses down and let him in. There was no reason for his chest to burn, no sense in clenching his teeth to the point of pain.

But the possessive Viking in him hated any man being near her, and he had to keep himself glued to the couch.

When Ella freed herself from Ricardo's arms, she was glowing. Tension washed away from Channing's body. He couldn't be angry at anyone who put a smile like that on her face.

Ella spread her arms to her sides. "Where've I been? In ninth-century Norway."

Ricardo bit his lower lip and narrowed his eyes at her. "Are you sure, chica?"

"I'm sure."

"It wasn't a setup...a sick reality show or something? Or brainwashing?"

Channing crossed his arms over his chest. "What did you think was happening when I disappeared after touching the golden spindle? That I was David Copperfield?"

The smile on Ella's face faded. "It wasn't a reality show. It was reality. I got shot by an arrow."

Ricardo and her family went still.

"You what?" barked Bryan.

"I'm fine." Ella went to Ted and wrapped her arm around his shoulders. "Channing helped me."

Ricardo's nostrils flared. "You goddamn motherfucker, how could you have let that happen?"

"Language, Ricardo." Gloria made big eyes at Ted.

Ted grinned. "Potty mouth."

"Sorry, Ted," Ricardo mumbled.

Ella approached the sideboard. "It wasn't Channing's fault." She opened a drawer and took out a comic book. "I was kept prisoner, and it happened when I escaped." She put the comic book on the dining room table in front of Ted, whose eyes shone as he opened it. "Channing treated my wound and brought us to his family. Without him I'd be dead."

Across the room, her gaze found his. There was so much love and heat and appreciation in her gorgeous blue eyes that Channing's throat clenched. His woman... He didn't need to worry about Ricardo. He just needed to worry about keeping her alive during Ragnarök.

Ricardo gave Channing a long, heavy look, then sighed. "Then I'm glad me risking my job paid off."

"Oh, shoot," Ella murmured. "They didn't fire you for losing Channing, did they?"

"Not yet. There are ten times as many criminals as cops, so every one of us counts."

Ella looked at Channing. He knew what she was asking. If they could tell Ricardo, Bryan, and Gloria everything.

Channing nodded. This was her family. He'd told his family in the Viking Age everything, and Ella should, too.

Ella told them the whole story. She told her dad about the Norns and the prophecy. She said as long as Channing lived, Ragnarök would end the world. Swallowing the fear as heavy as lead, Channing watched Bryan's reaction.

Bryan's gaze was as sharp as a blade. Gloria was shaking her head, mumbling that she couldn't believe any of that. Not Channing. All that nonsense belonged to novels and TV, not to real life. Ricardo stopped Ella several times, asking for details and staring in disbelief as she told them about her vision of the Norn.

It was getting darker and darker in the living room, the dim afternoon light seeping through the window like it was passing through a glacier, and Ted moved onto the sill of the bay window to read.

Ella finished her story with how they'd appeared in the Port of Boston. How they'd seen the port in the hands of the Boston Mafia.

There was a sudden flash outside the window, followed by the distant rumble of thunder. Then warm light flooded the living room, blinding Channing. The fridge in the kitchen burred angrily for a brief moment, then resumed its usual quiet droning.

"It's Rolf!" Ted exclaimed, then giggled. "He sent the lightning and now the power is back."

Gloria chuckled.

"Don't laugh, Mom," said Ted. "Lightning is made of power."

Gloria stood up. "I'm not laughing at you, hon. You're right, it is made of power. Though usually lightning storms knock the power out rather than turn it on. Speaking of, now that it's back, I can start dinner and make some tea or coffee. How about a cup of something warm, everyone?"

The thought of a warm liquid inside his body made Channing's stomach ache longingly. "I'd love some tea, Gloria," he said. "Thank you."

Ella stretched her neck. "Do you mind making coffee? Thank you, Gloria. I missed it so much."

"Nothing for me," said Ricardo, rubbing his chin.

Someone knocked on the front door. "Gloria! Bryan! Power is back on!"

The door opened and a short, round version of Bryan walked inside. "You need any—"

That must be Uncle Maurice, based on what Ella had told Channing about him. He stopped, staring at Ella. "You're back?" He ran towards the front door and yelled up the stairs, "Ella is back! She's back!"

Voices came from the second floor, then the pounding of several feet against the wooden stairs almost drowned out another rumble of thunder.

"Ella?!" boomed a tall middle-aged man with dark hair. He held a toddler on his hip. That must be Rob and his daughter, Pamela.

Ella beamed and jumped to her feet, and the incomers grew silent, looking her over.

She'd told him all about them. That Rob that had been wrongfully fired from Channing's port a few months ago. That Uncle Mo used to have a pub in downtown Boston, where only a few weeks ago, seeking shelter from another snowstorm, Ella and Channing had made love for the first time.

"What the hell are you two wearing?" asked a pregnant woman in her early thirties. Must be Stella, Rob's wife.

A short woman in her fifties came into the living room and touched Ella's Viking coat trimmed with fur. "Christ on a bike. It's not *that* cold out, is it? You look like you came from the Arctic. Where in God's name have you been?"

That was probably her aunt Cara.

A young woman, looking like she could be a college student, peered from behind Rob. That should be Fiona, Ella's cousin. She didn't say anything, but looked at Ella with curiosity, and at him with caution.

As the apartment filled with voices—people talking, asking questions—Channing followed Gloria into the kitchen to help her make tea and coffee.

Yellow light reflected from the window, shielding the white whirls of snow and flashes of lightning outside from Channing's sight, and Ragnarök seemed like a distant worry. If the TV worked and they could warm up food, thoughts of unrest and food shortages and the lack of medicine and the port being overrun by the Mafia seemed like fiction.

Just for a moment, Channing would allow himself to sit back on the couch in an old triple-decker next to the love of his life, drink hot tea, and talk to her family. Feel the warmth of the hearth that she brought to life in him, healing the aching wound, inch by inch, filling the emptiness in his hollow chest.

Tomorrow, they'd think of a plan.

He knew one thing.

Death was coming for him, closer with every second.

But if anyone could trick it, it would be him, the man who defied destiny. Because now he had someone to live for. And if he had Ella, he'd find a way to defeat Ragnarök itself.

THREE

It was after dinner, and the living room was filled with the aroma of pea soup. In the dated kitchen Ella had known every day of her life, water splashed and tableware clunked against the metal sink as Gloria washed dishes.

This was so different from the Viking Age, where servants first needed to gather huge amounts of snow and then thaw it in the cauldrons suspended over fire to have water for cleaning and scrubbing.

Here, Gloria wore rubber gloves. Back in the ninth century, dishwasher women's hands were red, dry, and raw.

How easy it was here—just turn the handle on the tap and you have warm, running water. Press a switch and light floods the room. In the Viking Age, getting light and warmth was a constant struggle of chopping wood and keeping the fire going.

Channing stood by Gloria's side, and the muscles on his broad back under her dad's shirt moved as he wiped the plates. Her dad's clothes were too tight, and Ella wondered if at any moment the seams would pop and tear.

Just seeing him alive and moving made happiness spill

through her like warm liquor. Her man. The man she could trust, the man who had crossed time for her, the man whom destiny had brought to her when she'd needed him the most. Yes, he was stubborn, and he could be controlling, but he had the biggest heart. She breathed easier next to him. Things made sense.

And now, here...in the kitchen...her Viking in a checkered shirt, with one towel on his shoulder and another one in his hand wiping dishes, he was as domestic as could be. It was easy to imagine the home they could have. The scent of him, the primal masculine tang of him mixed with his body wash. Sexy and big, both reliable and unpredictable. Loyal and ambitious. Confident and deeply vulnerable.

Ever since her mother had left, Ella had been empty. No one she knew had odd dreams, no one else could manipulate time, and no one else's mom had left them. Something had been wrong with Ella, with her odd powers and her strange dreams. And she couldn't talk about it.

Even with the house full of people, three families living under one roof in the triple-decker, she'd been lonely.

And so had Channing.

And together, they fit. She'd told him everything about herself, and he'd seen the worst of her, and he still loved her. He hadn't left. Only with him, did she not have that deep feeling of oddness and awkwardness.

For the first time, she didn't feel lonely. She felt accepted. She felt like she belonged.

She was relieved of wiping duty because of her shoulder wound, and Dad was drying the glasses next to her at the kitchen table. Ricardo and the extended family had stayed for dinner. Ella had told them she had been kidnapped and that Channing, with Ricardo's assistance, had managed to help her escape. She didn't like lying to them, but she didn't think talking about time travel and Ragnarök with Uncle Mo and his family would bring anything but confusion and disbelief.

After they left, Ella had put Ted to bed and watched him fall asleep, with her heart squeezing. The thunder and lightning storm had passed, though snow still fell, and Ted's room was quiet and still. She'd studied his full cheeks and relaxed as he breathed, the dark eyelashes fluttering as his eyes moved under their lids.

The end of the world chased her and Channing. They had escaped King Harald, and she had saved the life of the man she loved. But now that she saw her brother, still a child, so sweet and innocent, a dark thought came.

Was it worth it? Or should she have let the ax fall?

What about the lives of millions of children all over the world? Children like Ted who hadn't had a chance to live full lives?

She hated herself for thinking it. No, she told herself. She was a half Norn. The three Norns were the most powerful beings in the world. They defined peoples' destinies.

And Ella had some sort of powers from her Norn mother she didn't completely understand. But she knew she had to do something with them. If anyone could help the world, it was her and Channing.

Mindlessly, she sorted the clean cutlery into the drawer using her uninjured arm.

"So, Dad," Ella said. "Tell me how crazy I am. The whole end of the world thing. Ragnarök. My mom being a Norn. Tell me what you're thinking."

"What I'm thinking..." Bryan chuckled and shook his head. "What I'm thinking is that I'm a dying man, and if I fail to see the truth at my age, I'm a fool." He carefully put the glass down on the table and it clunked softly against the wood. "And I'm no fool."

Channing stopped wiping and looked at him over his shoulder. "So what? You believe us? About everything?"

Bryan shot him a hard look. "I believe you. Doesn't mean that I like it. But I believe you."

Ella placed a large kitchen knife into the utensil drawer. The knife blades, dull from time and use, reflected the yellow energy-saving light. Would she ever need to use them to protect her family against neighbors she'd grown up with? Against her own family who lived upstairs? They'd been nice enough today, but it would get worse. Hunger could make people do unspeakable things.

She put another knife into the drawer. "Even about Channing being the reason for Ragnarök?"

Bryan picked up the glass again. "I don't know that I agree with it. But I assume it can be possible, yes. The time machine you created, I can see the logic of how it would upset the Norns. You used science to do what their magic does. That might disturb reality or whatever. The nuclear reactor you got imported, it's dangerous, man."

Channing took another wet plate from Gloria's hands and froze for a moment. "I know."

The plate clunked loudly as he placed it on the growing pile, and everyone looked at him. "Exactly. You knew and yet you still endangered Boston by importing it." Bryan's voice rang with anger. "But blaming you alone for all the problems of the world is overkill. What do you think, Ella?"

Ella froze with a spoon in her hand.

"Now that we know your mother is a Norn, someone who defines destiny," Dad continued, "you're probably one of the best people to tell whether there's any truth in this."

Ella swallowed, feeling three pairs of eyes on her. The clanking of the dishes stopped. The buzzing of the fridge filled the kitchen.

She carefully placed the spoon in the drawer. "I don't know. I have no insights about that, Dad. Whatever I can do as a Norn, it's nothing about knowing or defining destiny."

Her dad leaned back in his wheelchair and looked at her from under eyelashes. "I think you're wrong."

She blinked. Channing turned to Bryan, slowly wiping the plate in a circular motion. "Why?"

Bryan looked at Gloria. "Sweetheart, I hope you don't mind me talking about Ella's mother."

Gloria threw a quick glance at him over her shoulder and pulled the plug out of the drain. Dirty water gurgled as it rushed down the pipes. "Tell them anything you want, hon."

Bryan took a long, deep breath, looking into space. "I know you were too little to remember, Ella. But I do. She always watched you. She would do her embroidery, and you were, of course, too young to try it yourself, but she'd tell you what she was working on. The image of Odin being hanged from that tree...the scenes from Ragnarök...and then that place, by the roots of Yggdrasil... I didn't know what significance it had back then. I just thought it was her way of telling you folk tales and keeping her Norwegian heritage alive. She loved that embroidery, and she told you about the Norns so many times... Perhaps there is some sort of clue in that embroidery."

With her chest tightening, Ella strained her mind, trying to bring back the memory. Her mother's icy blue eyes, shining, as her needle sank into the fabric back and forth, her lips moving. The golden sunlight in her blond hair, the mysterious herbal scent of her, like a field of wildflowers by the seaside.

But she couldn't remember her mother's words. "Like what, Dad?"

Dad narrowed his eyes, thinking. "We need to look at the embroidery..."

Gloria wiped her hands on the kitchen towel and threw it

onto the table. "I'll fetch it," she threw over her shoulder and rushed out of the kitchen without looking at anyone. Ella frowned at her dad. "Is she okay?"

Dad stared at the open door. "I don't know."

Gloria came back and shoved the embroidery into Ella's hands. "Here."

Then, with her eyes wet, she went to the door, but Ella caught her by the arm. "Gloria, what is it?"

"I...I just feel like... God, Ella, I've been worried sick about you. She left you, honey. Norn or not. Powers or not, she *left* you. You and Bryan. And it was me who raised you. Not her. It was me who took care of you and your dad. And now...you're talking like she's a goddess, like she's...everything."

Gloria's face reddened, and wrinkles deepened around her eyes as she fought tears. Dear Gloria, who had appeared in Ella's life three years after her mother disappeared. And Ella had despised her at first. No one could replace her mom, no one would ever...

But Gloria had tried. Endlessly caring, always nice, making thoughtful gifts and small gestures of friendship. Over the years, she had become, essentially, Ella's mother.

"Gloria..." Ella whispered and put down a spoon and the embroidery. "I love you. You're family."

Gloria sobbed and hid her face in her hands, and Ella wrapped her arms around Gloria's plump frame. She smelled like cooked vegetables, and like dish soap, and like home.

"It's just..." she whispered, shaking in Ella's arms. "Your dad's sick, and you disappeared, and we can barely find food, and I constantly worry about Ted..."

Ella felt a tear roll down her cheek. She was right. Dad was dying. Once he was gone, they'd have only each other.

"You're the best thing that happened to me and Dad," Ella whispered into her ear. "I'm sorry I made you worry."

Gloria sighed out, gently pulled away, and cupped Ella's cheek. Dark mascara glistened around Gloria's brown eyes. "I love you, too, honey. Let me know what I can do to help." She threw a glance at Channing. "Don't let my smiles fool you, young man. If you break her heart, I'll kill you."

Channing raised his eyebrows. "Yes, ma'am."

Gloria wiped her eyes and stepped back. "I'll go to bed..." Her eyes dropped on the embroidery that lay flat on the kitchen countertop. "They all have spindles, the three of them," she said. "I bet they can't do a thing without the spindles."

As Ella studied the embroidery with a frown, she noticed distantly that Gloria kissed her on the cheek, then Channing, then her dad and said goodbye and left the kitchen. Ella knew every inch of this embroidery—over the years, she'd looked at it so long at times, she was afraid she might have drilled holes in it with her eyes. If only she had known that one of the dark female figures who slouched over three golden spindles under the giant tree was her own mother. The two others were her aunts.

Under their feet was Urðarbrunnr, the well that fed the world tree Yggdrasil, which was a giant white ash tree. The dark, still water of the well reflected the three women and their spindles like a black mirror. Behind them was a beautiful golden mead hall. The water was supposed to be so healing and holy, and gods rode over the rainbow bridge Bifröst to hold court at the well. The Norns gathered water from Urðarbrunnr and mud and poured it over Yggdrasil so that the branches and the roots didn't rot.

I bet they can't do a thing without the spindles, Gloria had said.

Ella looked at Channing and then at her dad. "The time machine. It all started because Channing created a spindle of his own."

Dad narrowed his eyes and drummed his fingers against the table.

"Do you think Ragnarök wouldn't have happened if he hadn't?"

Channing's green eyes blazed. "I think so. But now the time machine is in the hands of the Mafia."

"We need to talk to Ricardo," said Ella. "Get the police to help."

Bryan shook his head. "Things have gotten so much worse since you left, Ella." He rolled his wheelchair to the counter, picked up the stack of clean plates Channing had just dried, and put them on his lap. "The police are as helpless as kittens with everything else going on. Keeping folks out of the supermarkets and warehouses is bad enough. Break-ins, robberies, more and more racketeering, and domestic abuse calls. It's bad."

Ella lifted her head. "Well then, we have our work carved out for us, Channing. We have to take back that time machine."

<h1 style="text-align:center">FOUR</h1>

Later that night, Channing lay facing Ella in her bed, stroking her hair as she slept.

The woman he loved was the daughter of a Norn...

Her eyes were closed, and soft white light of the snow falling outside illuminated her face. Her skin looked almost like porcelain against the olive skin that spoke to his dark heritage.

He still hadn't told her that Leo Esposito, the don of the Boston Mafia, was his grandfather. That his father had abused and raped his mother. Would she stay with him if she knew Channing was more entangled in the world of crime than she thought?

The house around them was silent, making Channing acutely aware of any sounds. The storm had quieted, and he could hear a few cars in the distance and shouts and cries of people. Upstairs, in her uncle Mo and her aunt Cara's apartment, the wooden floor creaked under someone's feet.

Back in the ninth century, there were no second floors, no windows, no central heating. Back in the ninth century, where his family had been left behind again.

Had his father survived? Had his sister and brother recovered from the smoke inhalation and burns?

The hole in his chest ached. The hole that would never be filled without them. His honorable father, his kind mother. He knew his brother would be a strong leader one day, taking his father's place as jarl. And his sister would be a feared warrior woman like she'd always wanted.

"In the morning," Ella whispered without opening her eyes, "we'll go back to the port."

Warmth spilled through his veins as he slid his hand down the curve of her waist. Hopefully, he'd have his own family one day with her. Children to worry about. Happy days with his wife for the rest of his life.

"Ella, the Mafia...we might get caught."

The memory of her in the arms of King Harald, the gun at her temple, burned Channing's inner vision. The terror of losing her, both hot and cold, urging him to move while paralyzing him at the same time. Never had he been so afraid in his life. He couldn't let that happen again.

She looked at him with her transparent eyes, like blue diamonds, sparkling in the silvery light. "What other choice do we have? If the spindle is how the Norns operate, we have to get closer to it. I don't know how, but the answer is with the spindle. I can feel it."

If she could feel that, what else could she feel? What else could she find out? Was there any way she'd learn about Channing's relationship with the head of the Mafia?

Though, logically, how would she find out unless Channing told her himself? No one knew. Even Leo didn't know. And Channing sure as hell didn't want her to learn he was the descendant of the biggest crime family in Boston.

He brushed his worry aside and kissed her on the nose. "If you feel it, then it must be right."

She gave a delighted smile that fired the warmth of the hearth in his chest and brought on a grin he couldn't stop.

"What are you going to do about the port?" she asked, more serious this time. "It's yours. They can't just take it."

His grin gone, he lay on his back and put one arm behind his head. The feel of Ella's soft pillows, the scent of clean bedsheets was pleasant but still odd after weeks of sleeping on the ground or straw mattresses and furs. "I don't really care about the port if the world is coming to an end." He looked at her and tucked a strand of hair behind her ear. "What about your job at the police department?"

She nestled her chin on his chest and planted a soft kiss. Her round breast pressed against his naked torso, and he growled.

"I have to go back," she said and planted another kiss. Her warmth, her silky skin, and her soft lips brought blood to his groin. "See if I can help. I can't just stand by and watch the world crumble. They need all the help they can get."

"Is this about the mortgage? I can take care of it."

She rose on her elbow and looked at him. "Yes, of course it's about the mortgage."

Ella's family had been struggling even before Ragnarök. Her income was the main source that kept a roof over their heads and food on the table. But despite the lack of money, years of love had made the triple-decker feel like a welcoming home. Her room was small and simple and feminine, a little whimsical like her. The dove-blue curtains on the window and the blue bedsheets reminded him of Ella's eyes. The two large photos on the wall were beautiful, though clearly taken by an amateur. The ocean was too blue, the sky almost milky white, and the rough pebble beach a little too brown. Was it on the coast of New England somewhere? Did she take the photos herself?

Even these colors reminded him of her...her blond hair, her blue eyes, her pale skin. A bookshelf stood in the corner, made of pale-yellow wood, with house plants between the books. A dresser stood next to a neat desk. Like the rest of the house, the furnishings weren't new. The surfaces were scratched, faded, and discolored in places. But the pieces were well-cared for, clearly there to last.

He brushed his knuckles down her arm. "I can take care of it. You are wounded. We need to concentrate on getting you healed, and—"

"No. I've been providing for my family all these years. Just because you showed up—"

He stopped. "Showed up? Is that how you think of me? Just showing up?"

"Of course not. I just mean I don't want to depend on you. I don't want to depend on anyone."

He pulled her up so that she straddled him. Her weight, her feminine curves, the feel of her round, firm ass made him hard. She moved her pelvis and wriggled against his erection, adding fire to his pleasure. By Odin, he was ready to take on the entire world as long as he could have her in his arms.

"Woman..." He ran his hands up and down her back. "I appreciate your independence, but you need to be reasonable. I can help. Don't refuse me."

She cupped his face. "I don't refuse *you*, you stubborn Viking. I just refuse to be anything but my own woman."

He shook his head. "My stubborn, beautiful female."

That was both what he loved about her and what frustrated him...her independence. Her strength. Despite his wealth, his physical strength, and his achievements, he didn't think he deserved as much respect as she did. She was the one serving people and protecting them.

She was the one he admired. She was the one he adored. Worshipped.

He let out a long breath. He needed to let go and let her be, no matter how hard it was for him. "Okay."

She smiled and pushed against his chest so that she sat straight up on top of him. She pulled her T-shirt up and over her head, and her breasts were right there in front of him. Her pale-pink nipples hardened against the translucent porcelain skin of her breasts. His cock hardened, too.

He stroked her hair. "You...this...you make me feel like I'm home."

She relaxed against him. Being careful not to disturb the still-healing wound on her bandaged shoulder, he cupped her healthy shoulder with his hand and sucked her nipple into his mouth. Her skin was velvety against his tongue.

She shivered, the movement barely noticeable, but he felt it right there—against his tongue and his lips and his chest.

Oh, Freya. Home...that's what she was.

Home.

Her scent, the feminine sweetness, her wet desire seeping through her pajama bottoms.

"Sweetheart," he murmured against her breast. "Let the world end." She arched her neck. "You are all that matters."

He dragged his tongue along her soft flesh, savoring the sweet taste of her clean skin, and licked the space between her breasts. A sound of pleasure escaped from her throat. She shivered again and looked down at him, her lips open, panting.

Her normally pale-blue eyes were like dark sapphires.

He eased her onto her back—she was as light and as flexible as a cat. She opened up to him, spreading her legs, still dressed in her pale-blue pajama bottoms. The sight of the clean bandage on her shoulder singed him with the thought of what pain she went through...what pain they went through together as he cleaned and cauterized her wound.

He moved down her stomach, switching between kissing, nibbling, and licking.

"My warrior queen." He dipped the tip of his tongue into her navel and swirled. She arched her spine against him.

"My Freya."

She moaned and pressed her hand against her mouth to stifle herself. Her legs wrapped around his shoulders.

"My everything..."

He reached her sex. The scent of it clean and pungent made his dick ache, his balls tighten.

"Channing..." she breathed out.

He looked up at her. "Yeah?"

"Please..."

He half growled, half purred. The need, the ache in her voice was just like his own. He loved to drive her wild like this. He'd always thought this would be amazing, knowing his woman, what she liked, and what she loved even more. Not a one-night stand with a person he'd never see again.

One woman who he'd know everything about. He gently spread her folds and licked her wet sex, and she gasped and shivered.

"That's right, sweetheart," he murmured, "beg, and ask, and hope, and tell me what you want."

"This..."

He licked her again, deeper.

"Oh, God, yes, this."

Every word touched his blood like fire touched gasoline. He wanted her so much, his mouth watered. He took her sex in his mouth. He licked and sucked, clinging to her, then pulling back. He caressed her thighs, massaging them with his hands, feeling them tremble under his fingers.

When the moans coming from her mouth were needy and urgent, and she started to scratch at his shoulders, as though trying to pull him up, she didn't need to say it out loud.

He knew what she needed. The same need pulled at him, hardening his cock into a goddamn rock.

He pulled open the drawer of her nightstand and took out a condom. With his hands stiff, he broke the wrapping and pulled it over his length. She watched him with her eyes dark, crazed, her beautiful breasts rising and falling with her quick breaths.

Fuck, he wanted her. Wanted to take her. Dominate her. Make her his, again and again and again. Had she not had her shoulder wound, he'd have turned her over and fucked her from behind. She loved it, but he didn't want her to strain her shoulder more than necessary.

He towered over her, positioned himself against her sleek entrance... She was so wet, she was dripping on her sheets. He slid inside her in one smooth motion. She gasped when he was balls-deep in her tight, hot, sleek depths, her arms and legs wrapping around his body, clinging to him like a koala.

He looked into her eyes, the color as deep and rich now as a fjord. "I love you, Ella. I'll always love you."

"I love you," she echoed.

I love you... The words that were like honey through his veins. Like life's essence.

Without breaking eye contact, he moved. Withdrew and plunged back in, watching pleasure color her cheeks pink, her lower lip reddening as she bit it with her pearly white teeth.

Fiery sweetness was spreading through his own body as he pounded into her. He wished he could throw away the goddamn condom and be with her skin to skin. But protecting her was more important than his own pleasure.

They were moaning now, in unison. They breathed one breath. She grew tighter and tighter around him.

She stiffened and cried out and bucked back, her chest pressing into his.

She was coming. The orgasm slammed through him in a single spasm that seemed to last an eternity. As he was unraveling, he had a sudden sense he wasn't himself anymore.

They were one. Somewhere in the waves of unraveling, he stopped existing as him and started existing as they. In a space that wasn't here or there.

A space that was home.

FIVE

Time slowed or stopped altogether. They lay, interconnected, both unable to sleep.

Channing was heavy and hot, and Ella's silky body was pressing him into her mattress.

Staring at her ceiling, his eyes were drawn to a crack that started behind the curtain. It was thick at one end, as though it was flowing into a sea, fed by a hundred invisible glaciers all around the ceiling.

Like a fjord.

The ninth century had never been far from his mind, and having just returned, he was now seeing imaginary fjords on ceilings. He clearly did need some sleep. But there was something from their time in the Viking Age that was haunting him, something that wouldn't let him rest. A moment when he'd thought he'd lost any chance with her. He didn't want old arguments to come between them. He wanted them to be like this— happy, entwined, forever.

The argument had been because he was a control freak. Even if he had a good reason. She had decided to stay in the ninth century to find out about her mother. She'd abandoned their initial plan to find a way to send her to the twenty-first century.

During the argument, he'd snapped at her. He had been worried she'd be in constant danger if she stayed with him. Ragnarök followed him like a loyal dog.

Like one of those wolves.

"I'm sorry for our argument back in the hut."

She sighed. "I'm sorry, too."

He rose to a sitting position and brought her into his arms. Her legs were wrapped around his waist, her arms around his neck. Her soft entrance was nudged against his erection. Freya, he was hard again for her, ready to be one with her again.

He stroked his knuckles down her cheek. "I love you, Ella. I meant every word I said about us back there. I want a life with you."

Her eyes softened as she smiled. "Or whatever is left of it."

He closed his eyes. "Look. This will not be the end. I refuse to submit to the prophecy. I'll never yield to this unjust destiny. Not when I just found you."

"Neither will I." She ran her fingers through his hair. "We're going to figure this out. Maybe I can use my powers to go back in time and change something."

"Something? What?"

"If the time machine is the problem, like my dad suggested, I might be able to stop it from being created."

He couldn't breathe. "Not if it would mean I'd never meet you."

"I'll find you."

"No," he said. "Because you won't have to lose me. Ella, you... I don't think you understand what you are to me."

She stopped breathing, too, her lips parted as her wide eyes drank him in. "What am I, Channing?"

"You're my soul. You're the essence of me. I will cross hundreds of years again and again for one moment with you. Maybe it's true that everything happens for a reason." He kissed her, drinking in the soft femininity of her lips, the scent of her, so dear and familiar, and vital. "You are the reason. Without you, nothing matters. Without you, let the world burn."

"Don't say that," she whispered, a tear rolling down her cheek.

Something blazed within him, anger stirring like in a cauldron set to boil. He recognized it. It was the battle rage of a warrior prepared to win or die. That was how he'd been his whole life. How his father had raised him. The need to fight and to bring victory was in his blood. Perhaps it was in the heritage of his biological father, too.

It wasn't just in battles. It was about business, too. The drive to achieve what he wanted, no matter what.

That was who he was. A warrior. A conqueror. A victor. He didn't surrender. Not to competitors. Not to destiny. Not to Ragnarök itself. Even if part of him understood others wanted him to.

"I'll save the world," he whispered. "For you. For us. For our future."

"There may not be any fu—"

"There will be," he said. "The time machine came from an idea. From one thought. I made it happen. I will make this happen, too. Because I love you."

Her eyes filled with the same blaze of hope that burned within his own heart.

"Back in the hut, I asked you if you would marry me in another life, if the circumstances had been different. Do you remember what you answered?"

"I remember."

"What did you say, Ella?"

She swallowed, her eyes glistening with emotion. "I said yes."

Her yes swept through his veins like a drug, charging every cell with electricity.

She smiled. God, he'd trade his arm for a chance to see her smile every day. A grin spread across his lips. "Then this is all I need. I will stop Ragnarök. I will make it possible for us to have a future—any future we want."

Stopping Ragnarök was impossible. Going against the Norns was madness.

Defying destiny was futile.

But he was the one who made the impossible possible. Thoughts of him holding his and Ella's children made his skin itch with the need to run out and do whatever it took to stop Ragnarök. The woman he loved was his, and she wanted a life with him.

They would have a future. The world would have a future.

He'd make it happen.

SIX

Ella closed the broken part of the welded fence behind her and it rattled. A hundred feet away, across the snowed-in port, two Mafia goons stopped.

Next to her, Channing froze, and she held her breath, crouching over the snow.

The men's backs were towards Ella and Channing.

The storm that had passed last night had left Boston more handicapped than ever before. There were few snowplows out due to the gas shortage. And because of the snow, countless accidents had happened on the highways and now dozens of cars blocked them, making it impossible for trucks to get through with supplies. At least planes flew again, and ships could dock now that the sea was calmer. But they weren't the only area or the only country struggling due to the weather. The snowstorm had even reached the southern states. Texas, one of the biggest agricultural producers, had lost most of its fruit and vegetable crops.

Thanks to panic buying and the disrupted food distribution

chain, the supermarkets were empty of fresh produce and meat, and only canned and dried products were available.

And as *Fimbulwinter* had just started, everything would only get worse.

Three years would pass without a summer and with no sun.

Great battles would devastate the world.

Greed would make brothers kill brothers and fathers and sons lose the bonds of their kinship...

That was how Norse sagas described *Fimbulwinter*.

Without turning, the two goons with rifles in their hands talked and then walked away. Ella let out a long breath and nodded at the next warehouse building. They ran, wading through the knee-deep snow. Ella's chest ached for air by the time they reached the warehouse. She leaned against the wall, panting.

"How far are we from building M05?" she asked Channing, who'd plastered himself against the wall, breathing calmly. Damned Viking. He'd grown up used to long, snowy winters for the first eighteen years of his life. "Please don't tell me we'll have to walk through this snow all the way."

He looked up. "Two more warehouses." He pointed to their left, where thick snow lay like whipped cream behind two buildings. At the back of the third warehouse, a truck was half snowed in. "This is the safest way."

Ella cursed and nodded. Where were the Viking Age, tennis-racket-style snowshoes when one needed them? Well, perhaps soon snowshoes would become the norm in the entire world. That probably wasn't something she should wish for.

"Okay." She nodded. "Let's go."

Raising their legs high, they struggled through the snow.

Earlier this morning, they'd gone to Channing's apartment building, where, as he'd correctly predicted, there were no power shortages. While he'd changed clothes, Ella had watched snowed-in Boston from the fifty-fifth floor. It was like looking at the world from the walls of an impenetrable castle. All the troubles had seemed far away, and as Channing had hugged her from behind and pressed her against his hard body, a sense of safety and warmth had spread through her. Ella admitted that if it came to it, Dad, Gloria, and Ted should move there.

They could have it all. Last night, Channing had infected her with hope, with his commitment to do this at any cost. The feeling was like an obsession, a feverish muscle chill. Her head ached, a distant migraine forming as a voice asked her if she was foolish to hope for a normal life during an apocalypse.

To truly allow herself to love the man who might need to die to stop it.

To consider marrying him.

To think about what eye color their future baby would have —green or icy blue? Would it be blond or brown-haired? Fair-skinned or olive-skinned? Girl or boy?

By the time they reached building Mo5, her lungs were burning, her shoulder ached, and a needle was piercing through her side.

"Stay behind me," Channing said as he dug through the snow next to the back door. After a few minutes, he retrieved a key.

As he unlocked the door, Ella took out her dad's old Glock. "No, babe, you stay behind me."

His chest rose and fell quickly. "Out of the question."

He walked into the warehouse, and she whispered angrily after him, "You are weaponless. You don't even have your sword!"

He didn't reply, and she walked after him. Inside, it was quiet and dark. Daylight poured through the skylight windows. The shelving units stood empty. Rows of them had fallen and lay leaning against each other like dominoes. The police had taken everything from this warehouse to inspect for evidence. As they moved from storage rack to storage rack closer to the opening in the floor into Channing's secret basement, Ella saw more and more bullet holes in the metal shelving units and the walls.

Her heart beat faster as she remembered the last time she'd been in this building—her fellow policemen being wounded by the Mafia and dying. Death had flown past her, too, in the rain of bullets. And when it was over, she'd touched the golden spindle and traveled back in time...

Light and snatches of muted voices flowed from the big square opening in the floor, which led into the basement. Shoot. She had been hoping the Mafia had just left the spindle alone and were carrying on with their drug business. Though they probably wouldn't have taken the two scientists hostage unless they wanted to use the time machine.

Channing stopped and turned to her with a deep frown on his face.

Let's go closer and listen, she mouthed.

He nodded, and slowly, soundlessly, they moved to the opening.

About ten feet away from the edge of the square hole, Ella saw the top of someone's head. A man stood on the stairs leading down into the basement. She pulled on Channing's winter coat to make him stop and pointed at the head with her gun.

He nodded and indicated a nearby shelving unit, where a few random tools and parts were still stacked. They pressed themselves to the wall next to it and peered around the corner.

CHANNING HELD HIS BREATH, listening to the shreds of voices that came from the basement.

"...when can you make it..." An older voice...Boston accent...more familiar than he'd like.

"...we can't promise..." A female voice...cool, collected, and almost clinical...Georgina!

"...whatever you need..."

He had to get closer. He felt it in his bones that the conversation happening downstairs was crucial. As important as taking his next breath. As vital to him as blood.

Stepping carefully, he walked out from behind the shelf and ignored Ella tugging at his sleeve to pull him back.

"Channing!" Her urgent whisper didn't stop him.

Nothing would stop him. Closer and closer to the edge he stepped, closer to the light. He could see the shoulders and back of a man now. A step closer, another...

There it was, thirty feet down in the basement—the spindle, standing on its axis, Norse runes and carvings of dragons and wolves knotted together through the threads of destiny. Next to it was Leonardo Esposito, as always in a perfect, tailored suit. His white hair was immaculate. His handsome, clean-shaven face was thoughtful.

Hating the thought, Channing could see the similarities between himself and his biological grandfather. The facial features, the bone structure, the skin tone.

Next to him was Georgina, not in a lab coat this time. Munchie stood protectively between her and Leo. And although Channing admired the heroism of his MIT scientist, if either of them would protect the other, Georgina had a better chance than Munchie against the Mafia. Her shoulders were straight, her chin high. Munchie was pale, his dark eyes wide on Esposito.

"Maybe this will persuade you to work faster," said Leo. He

pulled out his cell phone and tapped it a few times, then showed it to the two scientists.

Georgina pursed her full lips in a vicious, furious grimace. "You asshole. Leave my family out of this!"

Hearing Georgina curse was more distressing than seeing Leo next to the spindle. What did he want with Georgina and Munchie? To have them manufacture drugs? To make them use the nuclear reactor that powered the time machine for some more nefarious purpose? To get them to disassemble the spindle?

"I'm telling you, we need time to figure out how to send you to 2019."

No... Leo had realized what he could do with the spindle. But why would he want to go to 2019?

"You both are MIT graduates, I'm told," Esposito said calmly. "You designed this." He pointed at the spindle. "You made it to send people through time."

Esposito swiped left several times on the screen of his cell, then stopped and showed it to them. "This is my only son, Daniel. He was killed on his yacht in the summer of 2019. The killer kidnapped Dan's girlfriend, who was pregnant with my grandchild, and I haven't heard of them since."

Channing's heart chilled.

Loki's bloody spit. This couldn't be happening.

"I hope that you both will never know the pain of losing a child. There's nothing worse. So if time travel works, the only purpose in my life is to go back in time before my son's death and stop his killer. To have my family back together. To hold my grandchild's little hand."

Channing felt as though he had floated high above his body and was looking at himself standing in the shadows, listening to the worst thing that could happen to him unfold.

Channing's mother, Mia, had killed Daniel Esposito on

that yacht when his father, Hakon, had traveled in time to free her from the hands of a monster. That monster was Channing's biological father.

Months later, she'd traveled to be with Hakon in the ninth century and had given birth to Channing there.

If Leo prevented Daniel's death, everything would be undone. Channing would be born in the twenty-first century and would now be two years old, growing up in the Mafia, watching his mother being abused by Daniel.

He'd never know Vikings. He'd never meet Hakon, the man who'd raised him.

He'd never meet Ella, the love of his life.

He'd never cause Ragnarök.

Georgina straightened her back even farther. "I'm sorry for your loss, truly. But if you want your family, I trust you won't let anything happen to ours. We'll figure it out. Give us time."

Channing backed up, not feeling his legs. Something buzzed in his ears like a swarm of angry wasps. His vision blurred. Distantly, he knew he hit something hard with his back and a loud metallic bang exploded through the warehouse. Bullets pinged around him as the guard fired at him and Ella shot back.

Then the man yelled and something heavy thudded against the metal stairs leading into the basement. She must have hit the guy.

Channing came to his senses, and they both ran. As new bullets started hitting the walls and the shelves behind them, they rushed outside in the blinding whiteness and hobbled through the snow towards Channing's secret entrance into the port.

He couldn't let his biological father live because he couldn't let his mother go through years of abuse. He couldn't be part of the Mafia.

And he couldn't *not* meet Ella.

As he opened the broken part of the welded fence for Ella to crawl through, he knew what he had to do.

The only way to stop Ragnarök was to destroy the one thing that allowed him a chance to go back in time and see his family.

He had to destroy the time machine.

And for that, he had to do another impossible thing.

Something that might endanger his relationship with Ella.

Get inside the Mafia.

SEVEN

The next day...

"I LIKE what you've done with the place." Channing looked around his office in the Port of Boston.

Sitting on Channing's elegant couch with his long arm stretched across the back, Leonardo Esposito gestured for Channing to take a seat.

Technically, Esposito didn't change anything in the interior of the office. It was still the large, 400-square-foot space Channing had spent the majority of his time during the last six years.

The snowed-in port spread through the two walls of floor-to-ceiling windows meeting at the corner. Only two cranes out of ten were at work, lifting the containers off two ships. A single truck drove through an uncleared road. Dark figures of Mafia men stood around building M01, which, Channing guessed, Leo probably used to store and distribute the smuggled drugs.

Did the man even care about the food still being transported to Boston by sea? Did he have anyone who'd keep taking care of that? He still had van Beek, Channing's port manager, who'd been behind the smuggling all this time without Channing's knowledge.

Now that the whole world was cold and attacked by storms all over the globe, every country struggled. They couldn't afford to waste the little produce there was available, because it would be even less with time.

"Channing Hakonson," said Esposito, looking him over. Channing wore a suit, which was a little loose now. He'd lost weight during his trip to the Viking Age.

Suits were armor in the business world, and he was going to meet Esposito ready for battle.

Part of him was sorry he couldn't tell Ella the truth about his plan to get inside the Mafia. Instead, he'd told her he was going to work with his lawyer, Giana Kilpatrick, to do something legal to get the port back. A futile idea, to be perfectly honest. What did the law mean when there was no one to impose it on those who broke it? But Ella knew he needed Giana to clear his name as he was still charged with importing illegal nuclear substances, although the drug trafficking charges had been dropped.

"You're a little too late to talk about our arrangement," said Esposito. "I don't need you anymore. I have your port."

Channing walked towards him and stopped before the coffee table. The wall art made of interwoven driftwood pieces hung on the wall above Leonardo. It was the piece Channing had been particularly partial to. It reminded him of knotted Norse patterns that decorated the spindle, the rune stones, the longhouses, and the boats. The wall piece was like him, Norse past blended with the present.

Behind it was Channing's safe where Leonardo had planted a bag of cocaine. He'd done it because Channing had refused to work with him, refused to allow cocaine to be smuggled through his port with his authorization. So they'd done it without.

But the fact that Channing had cocaine in his safe convinced the police that he had been responsible for the smuggling all along. They'd arrested him, and he'd been charged with cocaine smuggling as well as smuggling of radioactive materials.

He was on his way to becoming an official criminal thanks to his grandfather dearest.

Who had no idea he was his grandfather.

His office smelled the same—cleaning products, wood, paper, and elegant air perfume sticks his assistant had picked up. However, with Leonardo sitting on the couch, this place was no longer Channing's.

It seemed empty. The glass walls overlooking the port looked fragile. The modern furniture—all chrome, white, and muted warm grays—dull, chosen by someone who wanted to appear more important than he was.

To fit in where he didn't belong.

"You don't have my port. It still belongs to me."

"On paper, yes," Esposito said and leaned to his side to retrieve his phone from the pocket of his suit jacket. "Shall we call the police and ask them to confirm? I'm sure they'd love to know the criminal that imported cocaine in an unauthorized nuclear reactor is back from having run away."

"Sure." Channing crossed his arms on his chest. He'd decided. There was no turning back. Even though he hated every association with this man, with this business, this was for Ella. This was for them. He was all in. He was desperate to get it done. Whatever it took. "Call the police and tell them to lock up your only grandson for life."

Leo's smug smile fell. "What did you say?"

Taking in a long breath, Channing sat in the white leather

armchair across from him. The words were like poison on his tongue. "I'm your grandson."

"My gran—" Esposito's face wrinkled. "You're out of your mind. That doesn't even work logically. I only had one son, and he'd have been as old as you."

The feverish need to do something scratched at his throat. Channing stood up and went to the sideboard, which held a carafe of water. The miniature golden spindle that Georgina and Munchie had used to do tests stood, gleaming, on the sideboard next to it.

He itched to touch it, run his fingertips down the smooth surface, feel the indents, the power of this thing that had given humans the ability to travel in time.

Instead, he poured some scotch into a glass, then gulped the whole thing in one go. He hated this. He hated walking into the den of a hungry lion, closing the door behind him, and throwing the key away.

But he had to.

He turned to face Esposito. "How did you find out about time travel?"

"Van Beek's men saw you disappear after that cop brought you to the spindle. They heard your two scientists talking about it. They didn't understand a lot, almost nothing. But they told van Beek, and he told me. And we hunted them down and... persuaded them to tell the truth."

"And you believed them?"

"I did."

"Why? Most people wouldn't. It's time travel."

Leo scoffed. "The sort of things that we used to convince them to talk...they were telling the truth. And then you disappeared. Three men saw you."

Channing poured another glass for himself and asked Leo if he wanted any, and he nodded at the bottle of whiskey.

"So then," Channing said as he poured. The sharp, smoky scent of scotch tickled his nostrils. "If you believe in time travel, how can you be so sure I can't be your grandson?"

He picked up both glasses and brought them over. As Leo stared at him with heavy, intense eyes, Channing put the whiskey glass on the table and pushed it towards Leo. Then he took his seat and sipped his drink, staring right back at Leo.

"What the hell are you talking about?" Leo barked.

"Daniel's pregnant girlfriend, Mia. She disappeared after his death, right? She was hiding from your bunch and then she traveled back in time, still pregnant with me to escape you and the Mafia. She gave birth to me in the ninth century in Norway, where I was raised as a Viking."

Shaking his head slightly in disbelief, he listened. His facial expression was as though Channing reeked of something foul.

"When I was eighteen, I had to travel forward in time, believe me, by no will of my own. And when I opened my eyes, I had actually arrived years before my conception. I'm thirty-two years old now, and yes, I look as old as your son, but I'm his spawn. Biologically."

Leo scoffed. "You think I believe this bullshit?"

Channing shrugged. "Don't believe me? I don't blame you. A simple DNA test then. You told me a while ago I reminded you of your son. If you dig deeper into my background, I'm sure you'll have questions."

Leo threw back his whiskey and stood up. "You motherfucker. Playing with an old man's grief. You think I'm an idiot?"

"I think you're many things, but an idiot isn't one of them."

"What do you want? Why this sappy story?"

Channing sighed out, leaned forward, and pressed his elbows into his knees. "I went back in time and saw my family. My mother. My father, the man who raised me. Hakon Ulfson. My brother and sister. My whole life I wanted nothing to do with you. But I had to come back here, into this time, because I knew I don't belong in the Viking Age anymore."

"Right." Esposito walked to the sideboard and poured more scotch into his glass.

Channing turned to him. "And if I want to live in this century, you are the only family I have."

Esposito's mouth curved down in a grief-stricken expression. He gulped the whiskey and put the glass down with a thud. "And?"

"And...I want in."

"I don't need you anymore."

"I want in, in the Mafia." Channing's teeth ground after he said that. "Daniel is dead. You want an heir. You want your family back. I am both of those things."

Leo said nothing, only glared at him from under his heavy eyebrows, then he poured another glass and drank it.

"I'm probably losing my mind," he said, "but I do see him in you. The eyes...something in your face..."

Channing's fists clenched in a helpless rage. He hated being compared to his biological father like it was a good thing. Like it was something to be proud of.

This was for Ella. For him and her. For the chance of *them*.

Leo put the glass down on the sideboard and walked to the glass door. "Fuck it. A DNA test. I'm sure the two MIT graduates can do it. These days, the whole world is going crazy. Why not believe a lunatic? Entertain an old man."

As Channing walked through the door, Esposito followed him. "But if the test is negative," Leo said, "you fucking bastard, I swear to God, you're a dead man."

They were by the elevator now, and Channing pressed the call button. "Let's go, Grandpa. There's nothing else I'd rather do."

EIGHT

Inside the central police station felt only a few degrees warmer than outside. Dirty snow turned into dirty mush as Ella walked down the hall and condensation rose from her mouth. The overhead lights were on but flickering. The station was like a market, busy and loud. People with their hands cuffed—or without—sat on the benches along the hall or stood, huddling for warmth.

Ella bet most of them didn't mind being arrested if the alternative was being out on the streets.

As she entered the space where her and Ricardo's desks stood, nostalgia stabbed her in the heart. Not much time had passed since she'd been here last, but it felt like it was a different life. There were only three cops inside the office equipped for twenty detectives. The rest must be out, dealing with the bullshit on the streets. Watching her colleagues leaning over their computers, talking on their phones, she wondered if she was making the right decision. If she wasn't distracting herself from the main job she should be doing—

learning to understand her powers, trying everything she could to stop Ragnarök.

And deep in her soul, she knew she was.

But this was helping, too. People needed protection. People needed order, especially when chaos was knocking on their doors like it was now.

It had never been as clear to her as it was yesterday, when she and Channing had broken into building Mo5, that the Mafia needed to be stopped. And not just because of the golden spindle.

Because they were bringing more crime, more suffering, more death.

Ricardo leaned over a paper next to a thug, stabbing it with his pen while yelling at the man. He looked up at her and stopped talking, a barely noticeable chuckle touching his face. "Detective O'Connor."

"Detective Sanchez." She nodded, standing next to Ricardo's desk.

The thug turned to her over his shoulder. He had a bald head and the word *Surtr* tattooed on the side of his scalp, the letters resembled Viking runes. *Surtr*...the name sounded familiar.

Ricardo leaned back. "Good to see you here."

She nodded, throwing a longing glance at her own desk, which stood right next to Ricardo's. Based on a new pencil case in the shape of a football and a photo of a family she didn't recognize, someone else had taken it. Two tall stacks of paperwork threatened to slide onto the grimy floor.

She looked around. "Things are bad, aren't they?"

"Yeah."

"Is Wilson in?" She glanced down the office to the door with fogged glass.

"Yes. Just returned."

"He knows I'm back?"

"I told him, yes. To make sure no resources were wasted there."

She nodded. "Not that anyone looked much besides you, probably."

Ricardo waved his arm around. "As you see, it's busy."

"Okay. Let me see if I can help."

She walked towards Wilson's office but kept thinking. *Surtr...Surtr...*

She looked back. Ricardo glared at the thug. "Pyromaniac, huh?" he asked.

"We were freezing," the man said.

"So you admit to arson."

Arson...*Surtr...*

Then she knew.

She walked back to stand behind Ricardo and to look at the guy. He had a meaty face and a meaty head, a big mouth, and an enormous nose.

"Why do you have that word tattooed on your head?" she asked.

He narrowed his eyes. "Surtr?"

"Yes. Surtr."

"Ella..." said Ricardo in a warning.

"What is it to you?"

"From Norse mythology, Surtr is a giant who would bring forth the flames that would burn the earth."

She was convinced she'd met Fenrir, the giant wolf who was one of Loki's children. He had dragged Channing out of a hole in the ice in the Viking Age, saving his life. And regular wolves kept following Channing, helping him for no apparent reason.

Could this guy be a representation of the giant Surtr himself?

"Surtr Enterprises is the biggest producer of explosives in the world," said Ricardo darkly. "Their headquarters are right here, in Quincy."

Something dark and cold turned in the pit of Ella's gut.

"Do you work there?" Ella asked.

"I work there."

"As what?"

"As a mechanic."

"Why would you have the name of the company you work for tattooed on your head?" Ella hissed, acid in her throat.

He chuckled and leaned back, crossing his arms. "Different people have different beliefs. I believe it's time to see the world burn."

His deep-set eyes shone darkly from their sockets, making a shiver run over Ella's skin.

She looked at Ricardo. "Is he a known arsonist?"

Ricardo sighed out and shook his head. "No. First offense." He raised his voice. "You know you're facing life in prison!"

The man chuckled again. "Name's Sean Gleeson. And if I wanted to commit arson, I could have burned the entire city."

The door to Wilson's office opened and, red-faced and furious, he marched out, fists clenched. His gaze fell on Ella, and his frown deepened. He stopped. "O'Connor. Why are you here? I have no time for you. Just leave your report of where you disappeared to and go."

Ella stepped forward. "I came back to work."

"What work, O'Connor? Is Hakonson behind bars? No. You failed."

Ricardo stood. "That's unfair, sir. She got him arrested."

"And you let him slip through your fingers, Sanchez. It's a miracle you have a job, so you really have no place to talk."

Pushing her anger down, Ella cleared her throat. "Sir, with

all due respect, you need all the help you can get. I am still a detective, aren't I?"

Wilson crossed his arms over his chest and threw her a sharp look. "Only because I didn't get around to filing the paperwork. Where have you been? How did you just disappear?"

She and Ricardo exchanged a warning glance. They hadn't discussed how to explain her absence, but she had thought it through. Clearly, she couldn't tell Wilson about time travel, Vikings, and Channing being the reason for Ragnarök.

So she had to lie. "The Mafia abducted me, sir."

Wilson frowned. "Oh? Witnesses claim one moment you stood there, the next you were gone."

"It was a trick. I'm not sure what happened as I lost consciousness. All I know is I woke up one day and found myself being held captive in a basement." She undid her shirt and pulled the right sleeve down enough to show the bandage on her shoulder. Wilson frowned.

"They tortured me for information about what we know about them. And who we are after."

A grimace of empathy crossed Wilson's face. "You okay?"

"I'm fine. There will be a nasty burn scar, but I'm told it won't impair the use of my arm."

"They *burned* you? Good God. And what did you tell them?"

"Nothing, sir."

"Hm." He looked her up and down, clearly doubting. "A woman? Said nothing?"

Ricardo took a step and raised his hand. "Sir, with all due respect—"

"Ricardo, please," she said. Sometimes Ricardo needed a reminder she was quite capable of fighting her own battles. "Yes. I am a woman. I'm also a police officer, an excellent shot"

—and a half Norn who can do stuff with time—"and can bear more than most men. Didn't tell them anything, sir."

"How did you get out?"

"The goons were distracted, and I got free and fought my way out of there." Would he be satisfied with such a vague explanation?

Wilson's phone buzzed, and he looked at the screen, his frown deepening. "Goddamn it."

Without giving her another glance, he walked out, but she called after him.

"Captain Wilson, sir!"

He turned with a sigh. "What?"

"Will you let me come back? All I want is to get back to work and be useful."

He took in a deep breath. "All right. We need all the hands we can get. But once this insanity"—he waved his arms around him—"ends, I expect a full report on what happened and if you found out anything useful. For now, start on Sanchez's cases. Everyone's swamped. Criminals are getting stronger. There are rumors of illegal weapons shipments, unregistered firearms on the streets. The Mafia. The Irish mob. The goddamn street gangs. They're the ones running things these days. The FBI can't do anything, either. Have you heard about DC?"

"No," said Ricardo.

"Folks storming the goddamn White House right now. Mark my word, we'll be looking at martial law soon if we can't regain control."

Ella bit her lip. Fear trickled down her spine. Martial law meant anything went as long as it was for the good of order. Freedoms would be restricted, things would be taken away from people, and the military could use whatever weapons and force were necessary to establish order.

Oh, God, and what about Channing? He was still a

suspect. He had committed a crime. And he would have to face the consequences.

And Wilson would still expect her to deal with him, once all of this was over.

Channing was working with his lawyer on clearing his name, and Giana would defend him in court once the date was set.

"So then let's make sure it doesn't come to that," Ella said.

"Let's start with the Mafia," Wilson said. "They took over the port. They control the supply of goods, fuel, and food into the city."

"I'm on it, Captain," Ella responded.

"Finish with this guy." Wilson nodded at the tattooed thug. "And get to work. Welcome back, Detective O'Connor. I hope you won't regret returning."

NINE

After hastily filing the necessary paperwork, Ella got her badge back and her gun. Then she spent the day responding to 911 calls and issuing fines and warnings. The officers on duty had been instructed to bring in only the most severe cases as holding cells were limited and they were already at three times their legal capacity.

And there was so much paperwork. It was fine while the power lasted. But in the afternoon, the power was out for two hours, and she had to go old school, filling out reports with pen and paper.

Ricardo had been out on the streets, making sure order was kept as much as it was possible. The usual protocol of cops working as partners had been broken to deal with the unprecedented number of cases.

The usual shift times didn't apply anymore, either. Her shift was supposed to be over at 7 p.m., but she stayed later. So did every other cop.

It was only when Channing called to say he was going to pick her up in five minutes that she reluctantly rubbed her eyes, saved her report, and leaned back in her chair, willing the ache in her shoulder and the spinning in her head to go away.

She said goodbye to Ricardo, who threw a longing glance at her as she walked out, which she chose to interpret as his desire to go home like she was.

But once she sat in Channing's SUV, the exhaustion of the day pressed in around her. She'd taken some painkillers back in the office, but they hadn't kicked in yet.

"Hi," he said, and she melted.

His car smelled of him, delicious scents of the sea and wood and leather. She felt as if she were plunging back into the ninth century. Only two days ago, they had returned from the Viking Age. Two days, and she found herself aching for the simplicity of life back there, the importance of stone and iron and wood.

The connection to her roots.

He was that for her.

"Hi, my Viking." She smiled as she kissed him. He grinned back a happy smile she'd seen only a handful of times on him as he rolled out of the parking lot. The nickname was new and intimate and idyllic. As they drove down the dark Boston streets, she realized she'd given in to him more than she'd ever imagined she could. She was vulnerable and open, and her soul and her happiness were completely at his mercy.

"How was your day?" he said, an edge of playfulness in his voice.

The dashboard of the car illuminated his handsome face—the high cheekbones, the straight, Roman nose—making his eyes obsidian as he looked into the winter night beyond the headlights.

"Don't ask." She sighed. "Let's just say I'm glad I'm doing something to help with the chaos."

He laid his hand on hers and squeezed. "I'm sure it's helping more than you know."

She thawed from his touch, from his words. The car's heat vent was blasting her legs, and, slowly, she relaxed into this heaven of Channing sitting right next to her, squeezing her hand. She felt ready to take on anything.

Anything like dinner.

"Gloria texted me earlier," she said. "Asked me to pick up some groceries for dinner."

"I thought we were going to my place," he said. "I want to have you all to myself."

The need in his voice was an intoxication weakening her legs.

"We still can," she murmured. "We can get them the groceries and go back to your place."

He looked at her briefly. The need in his gaze was a dark touch on her skin. "I like that plan."

"How was your day? Did you make any progress?"

His face lost the relaxed, playful expression. "I met with Giana today. Lots of paperwork first. Fucking waste of time if you ask me. The court date is in eight months. The world will either be dead by then or I will be."

"Channing, don't say that."

"Anyway. There's stuff that I can do legally to the Mafia, but I wanted to see if I could find a solution with them without the cops and without the lawyers. I had a meeting with Leo Esposito."

A worm of worry twisted in her gut. "I don't like it."

"Neither do I. But that's what I need to do."

They arrived at the New Family Max store three blocks away from Ripley Street. As the car came to a soft halt in the indigo-golden darkness under the parking lot lights, Ella got out. The Glock attached to her belt under her jacket felt heavier than usual after being without a gun for so long.

A small car that had driven into the parking lot after them

stopped right in the middle of the lane. The woman visible through the windows moved her hand jerkily, clearly struggling to get the car going.

"You go," said Channing. "I'll see if I can help her and then join you."

"Okay." She kissed him on the cheek. "I have the list."

As she walked towards the little grocery shop, the packed snow under her feet felt frozen solid. The condensation pumped out of her mouth as she closed the zip of her jacket up to her face. The brightly lit windows of the store threw yellow squares on the snow.

While Gloria had asked her to buy a bunch of things, the most important of which had been bread and milk and meat, Ella found only cans of corned beef, beans, and corn. For the most part, the shelves were empty. There were several customers in the shop already, and Ella felt a stupid sense of competition for the five cans of expired corn that were left on the shelf.

But she took only two.

When she walked out with a single thin paper bag, groups of men had gathered around the supermarket, smoking, huddling into their padded jackets.

As she passed by, five of them separated from the crowd and walked to her with a cocky swagger and menace on their faces. Snow crunched under their feet and condensation pumped out in clouds as they followed her.

She put her hand on her Glock.

But when the first man was close enough that she could see his face, she relaxed. It was Nick Murphy, the guy from one of three triple-deckers down the street. They'd gone on a couple of dates. But she'd broken things off when she'd realized he may be involved with Freddie Dublin's mob.

As an Irish descendant growing up in Dorchester, the

cliché, "every family has a priest, a cop, and a mobster" hit way too close to home. Everybody on the street knew who might be involved with the mob. But those same "bad guys" bought groceries for old ladies and protected the kids who were being bullied.

When Nick recognized her, his eyebrows lifted up to his hairline. He looked back at his buddies with a grin. Among them were more familiar faces from her street. Uncle Mo had taught one or two of them how to box in the backyard when they were her age.

"It's Ella O'Connor," Nick proclaimed and scooped her into his arms. "I heard you were gone. Glad to see you."

The others greeted her with polite smiles and nods. She gave a faint chuckle, looking them over. "Watcha doing, boys?"

"Are you still a cop?" Nick asked.

Ella crossed her arms over her chest, hugging her paper bag. "Why?"

One of the men mumbled, "Wouldn't matter even if she was."

Nick leaned closer to her. "There's no more fresh meat in the store, but Freddie Dublin has a stock of corned beef. Other food, too. His men have been gathering it for days. Should be enough to get us all through the storms. If Bryan wants some..."

Ella's mouth flew open. "You're kidding. People starve on the streets, and you just take the food away?"

Nick gave her a cold look. "We didn't take it away from people on the streets. We robbed the warehouses."

The faces of the men suddenly lost their cockiness. A shadow grew by her side.

"Is everything all right?" Channing's voice, like always, brought a warm shiver through her body. She didn't need his protection.

But that didn't mean she didn't enjoy the astonishment on

Nick's and his boys' faces when her Viking appeared by her side.

She turned her head to him. His profile was a stone mask, his eyes hard steel on the men in front of him. He was weaponless. They, no doubt, had guns. And yet he was the wolf, and they were trembling rabbits.

"Everything's fine, Channing," she said and rustled the paper bag. "Got all I need. Let's go."

She and Channing turned to walk away.

"Ella…" Nick said.

She looked at him over her shoulder. "Not a word more, Nick. I wish I were on duty to arrest all of you."

As she and Channing walked towards the car, angry shouts of "Fuck you" and "Fucking police bitch" and jeering laughter followed her. She shouldn't make new enemies.

She felt Channing's tension like her own. "Not just the Mafia is getting stronger, but the Irish mob, too."

"Are they in the mob?" he asked.

"Yeah. The Irish and the Mafia are the strongest criminal organizations. There are also several street gangs. With so much upheaval, they might join the big players, or unite among themselves…"

Channing took the grocery bag from her hands and opened the door of his SUV for her. "Shit."

She climbed in and waited for him to get inside, too. Once he was in, he put the grocery bag on the back seat. He started the car, and she rubbed her hands together in front of the blasting heat vent.

"It's not just Boston," she said. "I heard in the station today it's also New York, Philadelphia, Washington, Chicago, Los Angeles… Everywhere in the United States and the world, crime is rising exponentially. The police, the FBI, the CIA, the army aren't enough."

Channing rested his wrist on the wheel and looked in front of him thoughtfully. "I heard the news today. They keep talking about the police failing, people being murdered, people over-dosing, street fights, and riots. Not just here. Around the globe."

"This has to stop," she whispered. "I need to figure out how to use my powers to end Ragnarök."

For them, Channing had told her. Because he loved her. Because she loved him. Because they wanted their future together.

He drove the car out of the parking lot. As his lights brushed past Nick and his gang, their menacing faces flashed white against black.

His voice was way too soft as he asked, "Is that Nick, your ex?"

Ella choked on her breath. "My ex?"

"When I came to your house for the first time, Ted asked me if I was Nick. Is that the Nick he meant?"

The tension in his voice was like the rumbling of a train. Distant and low, but powerful and imminent.

"Um..." She looked at his profile, trying to read him, under-stand what was going on in his head. "I dated him a few times. That's all."

He kept staring at the dark street crawling slowly in front of him. "That's all?"

"Yeah. We grew up on the same street. Went to the same school. Played together. He knows Rob..."

"He knows Rob..."

"Yes. The whole family."

"But Ted didn't know what he looked like."

"Ted didn't see a lot of him. And he tends to remember only those he cares about."

His knuckles whitened as he gripped the wheel tighter. "Did you kiss Nick?"

Her stomach dropped. "Why would you want to know that?"

"Because you're mine, and I want to know if your ex kissed you."

She was his... Her insides quivered more than she thought they would.

"He's not my ex."

"If he dated you, he is as far as I'm concerned. He may still have feelings for you. He could be a danger to you."

Yes, he had kissed her. But no way she was going to say that to Channing.

"It was just a few dates," she said. "I realized very quickly I could never be with him. The rest doesn't concern you. I don't ask you about your exes."

He didn't say anything. They arrived, and he parked the car. Without another word, she got the groceries and brought them into the triple-decker. A few minutes later, she returned to the car, where Channing was still staring in front of him.

As they drove to his place, Ella sighed. "He's nothing to me. You should know that."

He didn't reply for some time. Then his voice came, as cold as an ice sheet. "I know Nick isn't a threat to what we have. But if he does anything to harm you, I'll kill him."

TEN

The next day, Ella asked for an afternoon off work to take her dad to the hospital. She drove Dad and Ted back home after the appointment. It was the first consultation with Dad's doctor, and he'd reluctantly agreed to start chemotherapy with the new experimental drug. Everything had been delayed because the hospital was overwhelmed with an uncommon number of frostbite cases, stab wounds, and gunshot wounds.

Dad had gone with the condition that she'd have her shoulder wound checked, too. The shocked ER doctor had said it had healed nicely and to take it easy, then had a nurse re-dress her wound.

During the drive home on one of the narrow, snowed-in Southie streets she saw them.

As they passed by the projects, three-story houses that looked like a prison block, something furry and gray flashed in her peripheral vision on the sidewalk. Wolves again. Under the mural of colorful, diverse faces, with the big black words *Faith, Hope,* and *Justice* on the red brick wall, wolves were eating something.

Something dressed in a puffy red jacket.

She hit the brakes so fast, Dad jolted forward in his wheelchair at the back of the van. They skidded on the icy street for a few seconds before coming to a stop.

"Ella!" Dad exclaimed.

"Sorry…" Ella took her Glock out. "Wait here."

After only a few days back on the job, the feel of it had become more familiar than ever. She'd had to draw her gun as many times in the past few days as she had in her entire career before Ragnarök.

"Ella?" Ted's worried voice called from the back seat closest to Dad's chair.

As she opened her driver's door, Dad peered out through the nearest window, trying to see what she was looking at. "Don't you dare. Those are wild animals."

"That person might still be alive," she spat. "Ted, I might need to shoot, so cover your ears. But everything will be all right. I just want to help that person. Okay?"

Ted nodded and covered his ears and closed his eyes tight.

"Ella, leave this. Look at him!" Dad put his arm on Ted's shoulder and patted him.

With a heavy heart, she remembered the day in the port when Channing, she, and Ted were surrounded by a hungry mob and she'd had to shoot. How Ted had screamed, terrified, unable to process what was happening.

She'd had to use her gun to save Channing's life. She had to help this person, too. It seemed she couldn't go anywhere without a gun these days.

She climbed out of the car and raised the gun, sending a warning shot into the gray sky.

The wolves darted away, disappearing down a tiny alley between two buildings. Their jaws were red with blood.

Now that the wolves were gone, she could see clearly. The

body couldn't be alive. The stomach was ripped open, and the face was half eaten.

"Dad, don't let him see," she cried.

Maybe she could go back in time and save that person... She tensed, calling something within her, remembering the moments when she'd been able to turn back time while awake and while she dreamed. Silently calling for something to stop time and rewind...

But nothing happened. A raven cawed somewhere. A wolf howled not far off. A car whirred past a block or so away. An empty swing creaked, moved by a sudden gust of wind.

In the windows, curtains shifted and faces peered at her. Cold horror dripped down her spine. This was daylight. This was a street where people lived.

This had happened on their watch. "What's wrong with you people?" she yelled. "Why didn't you save this person?"

But the answer was obvious. There was a brown paper grocery bag next to the dead body. A loaf of bread, a six pack of yogurt, and a carton of shelf-stable milk lay on the ground. Like vultures, people waited for the wolves to leave so that they could get the food.

Her eyes burned with sadness. "Go take your spoils," she whispered as she climbed back into the car.

She closed the door and started the ignition. As she drove, Dad continued to stare out the window at the dead body. "I didn't know wolves had started attacking people."

In the rearview mirror, Ella saw people run out of the houses and hurry towards the groceries. They snatched the food. Two pulled the loaf of bread in opposite directions. One of them let it go and hit the other in the face.

Ella focused her eyes on the road. Tears burned at the backs of her eyes. Anger at people scalded her gut.

Ella saw in the mirror that Dad shook Ted's shoulder and he opened his eyes. "It's okay, it's over," Dad said.

"Fucking people..." Ella muttered.

The worst thing about Ragnarök wasn't the storms and the lack of food and disruption of power.

It was that it brought out the worst in people. They lost the human part and what was left were just beings.

Animals. Like those wolves.

Her fingers ached from how hard she held the wheel, and she unclenched them, stretching them out. "We need the spindle."

Dad cracked his knuckles. "Look. I was thinking. Maybe it doesn't need to be golden. I can't make you a golden one. But I will make you a wooden one."

A wooden one? "I'm not sure it'll work. I don't want you to waste your time."

"I'm not doing anything, anyway. Let me be useful. My dad taught me a bit of wood carving when I was a kid."

She doubted it would work, but...he was right. She could try. "What the hell." She looked at her dad in the mirror and smiled warmly. "Thanks, Dad."

"I want to help!" said Ted.

As she drove, she hoped Channing was making progress getting the port back. The port that housed the golden spindle they desperately needed. She doubted a wooden spindle would help, but it would be something to practice with, anyway.

By that evening, Dad presented Ella a wooden spindle. Rob, who was handy and had nothing to do, volunteered to help. Dad and Ted then carved out some rough patterns and the runes according to Channing's notes he'd emailed Ella. The runes were not as precise as the ones on the time machine spindle, but they were there.

"New hobby, Ella?" Rob asked as he held the spindle out for her.

She didn't take it. What if she touched it and disappeared back in time again? "Something like that."

After a few moments of silence, Dad said, "Just put it on the table, will you?"

Rob cleared his throat and carefully placed the spindle on the dinner table. "O-kay..." It rolled gently and then stopped. "Ahem. Won't you try it? I'd like to see if it works. Never made one before."

Ella's fingers went icy cold. The memory of the nothingness and darkness engulfing her as she was sucked into another time was like a distant migraine.

"Um." She took a step closer. She hadn't thought she'd be like this, so hesitant, so afraid. "I don't have any wool. Need to get some first."

Rob put his hands into his pockets. "Oh. You just sounded like this was urgent."

"It is. I'll try it and let you know, okay?" She gave him a reassuring smile. "Thank you so much for your help."

"Ah, no problem. Good for you to learn to spin these days. Who knows if we'll be able to buy clothes in the next couple of months. Have you heard? China and Taiwan closed their clothing factories."

Ella took another step closer to the table. "I haven't."

"Yeah. Because of the storms everywhere, fuel can't be delivered. Fabric can't be made without the raw materials."

Good grief. It was getting worse. If this spindle was the answer, she was wasting time. She should just take it and see what happened. But if she did end up traveling in time, she wanted to say goodbye first. She never got to last time.

Just when Ella wanted to say something, Rob blurted out, "Uncle Bryan, Ella, you probably won't approve...but...Freddie

Dublin's looking for men. Nick approached me about joining them this morning."

Horror dragged an icicle down Ella's spine. "Rob...no. Freddie's mob is stealing food from warehouses, keeping it from reaching people who need it."

Rob's face lost its weak smile. "We need food, Ella. My pregnant wife, my toddler, and my unborn child need it. So do my parents and my sister and so do you guys."

Dad rolled his wheelchair closer. "Rob—"

"No!" Rob raised his hand, stopping Bryan. "Do you know what it's like to be a grown man and not be able to provide for your family?"

Dad's expression darkened. "I do."

Rob's face reddened. "Sorry, I didn't mean—I know you do, of course, but—"

Bryan pointed at Rob. "You think I haven't wished every day of my life that I had dodged that bullet back then? That I had hidden behind that goddamn corner like a careful cop would and not tried to impress my superiors by being cocky and disregarding the safety protocols?"

Ella blinked. "Dad...I didn't know..."

"I wish I wasn't stuck in this damn wheelchair." He looked at Rob. "But I can't change it. And you won't be able to change it either if you make the wrong choice."

Rob let out a long sigh. "I didn't mean to point out your circumstances, Uncle Bryan. It's not your fault what happened to you."

"Don't do this, Rob," Bryan said. "There are other ways to survive."

Rob scrubbed a hand through his hair and looked at Ella. "But how?"

The police needed to step in and stop the criminal organizations from hoarding the food supply. While she was learning to use her powers, she needed to help in more practical ways.

"We'll find a way, Rob. You still have food in the fridge, right? You guys aren't hungry, are you?"

"Well...no. Thanks to you, of course. But one day, we won't be able to buy anything anymore. And not just because of money. Because there'll be nothing left in the stores. Everything will be in the hands of the strongest. The richest."

And the strongest and the richest in Boston now were the Mafia, the Irish mob, and the gangs.

They were the wolves that feasted on weak people. They were the giants that fought and won against the gods.

Ella grabbed the back of the chair in front of her and leaned on it. "Maybe you're right. But if anything makes them rich and strong, it's us. It's choices like these. The O'Connors have always stood on the side of justice and order. That's why we are cops, honest business owners, and hardworking fathers like you."

And one-half Norn...

"We take care of one another," she continued. "We get creative. We keep our heads high. But we don't sell ourselves to the world of crime. You'll never forgive yourself if you do."

Rob looked down and nodded.

"Promise you'll refuse them."

"I will."

Ella came to him and clapped him on the shoulder. "Good. And I promise you, I have a plan."

When Rob was finally gone, Ella felt like she could speak freely.

"Did you mean it when you said you wished you weren't in the wheelchair?" she asked her dad.

"Of course I wish it, Ella. I wish I could help you. I wish I could protect you and Gloria and Ted. I wish I could relieve you from taking care of us. It's what a father is supposed to do, what I want to do for you guys."

He did so well in the chair. He had adapted. Yet she knew it hadn't been easy for him. He'd been frustrated with his limitations. She'd seen his self-destructiveness, his bitterness, his despair get worse with age. Having to abandon his role of provider and protector had been a shock to him. A shock he'd never fully recovered from. A new life he'd never really accepted. The talk they'd had a few weeks ago, when he'd said he didn't want to live anymore, had chilled her to her bones.

If the Norns did define destiny and everything had been on that tapestry before people were born...how could they have woven this hard life for him? And what about that poor person in the red jacket, killed by wolves on a city street?

She didn't know anything about destiny, but what she had seen seemed cruel. She wished she could change things. She might be the only person who could. But she didn't even know how to activate her powers. Every time she'd been able to control time in her waking life, it had been in response to danger—when she'd had to act or Channing would have died.

But when she'd touched the time machine, it wasn't because Channing had been in danger. Maybe it was because of what she'd said...something about traveling in time.

She looked at her dad. The buzzing of the fridge in the adjacent kitchen was loud. Their old clock ticked. Dad was solemn in the dim yellow lights of the living room. Ted hummed through the wall in his room as he played. "I love you, Dad. If this works and I am suddenly gone, just know that I love you. And you've always been my hero."

Dad's face straightened. "Ella—"

She came to stand next to the table, her hand over the spindle. "I wish I could travel in time."

She grabbed it.

ELEVEN

The same night...

LEANING against the column with a martini in his hand, Channing counted eight adults in the room. Leo had gathered the members of the family to either make an example of him— in which case, he'd be carried out of here dead...

Or to introduce him as his heir.

Either way, Channing wouldn't leave this house the same man.

The table in Leo Esposito's dining area was set for ten people, and an additional small table was set for five children. Yelling and squealing in delight, three boys and two girls between the ages of four and ten ran around the living room, which was full of classic furniture and art hanging on the marble walls. The only two women present were beautiful, well-groomed, and thin and talked to each other quietly, occasionally throwing curious glances at Channing and shushing the children.

Leo was discussing something with the five men standing next to the round bar. The painting he'd been working on the last time Channing was here was still unfinished, though it had gained more dark tones in the sky, showing the storm that was coming towards the light beach and the lonely sailboat.

One of the children, a four-year-old blond girl in a pink tutu, ran away from an eight-year-old boy who chased her with a glowing sword, a pirate patch on his eye. Giggling, she ran with her head turned back towards her chaser, past a coffee table in the middle of the conversation nook.

"Chloe!" cried one of the women, and Channing looked at the little girl. "Matteo! Slow down!"

But she didn't. And the boy didn't. It reminded Channing, painfully, of how he'd played with his own brother and sister growing up in the Viking Age. How they'd fought with wooden swords, how his own mother had yelled for him to slow down and to be careful.

The girl wasn't listening. In a typical child's ecstasy, she ran. Channing saw it before she did. The three steps leading out of the conversation pit.

"Chloe!" yelled the woman again.

And even though Channing was ten steps away and would never reach her in time, he darted forward to stop her from the fall.

But Leo Esposito reacted faster. He was the closest, but deep in conversation. Chloe's foot caught at the first step, and she fell forward, towards the sharp marble corners of the remaining steps. Despite his age, Leo sank to the ground with a grunt of pain and caught her. He swung her up and steadied her on the floor.

"Goddamn knees..." he muttered under his breath. "You okay, Chloe?"

"I'm fine, Grandpa."

Grandpa... What did that make her for Channing?

Leo looked at him while speaking to the little girl. "I'm not your grandpa, dear."

Chloe sat down on the step, panting. "But if you're my grandpa Joe's brother, you must be my grandpa, too."

Joe "Olive" had similar features to Leo, but rather than being lean like his brother, he was as round as an olive. He was the loudest one in the room besides the children, making jokes about hobos on the streets and bestiality that had Channing's hands clenching into fists.

"He's called your great-uncle, Chloe," said Sam. Fred and Sam were twins, middle-aged muscular men with the faces of alcoholics, obvious from their puffy noses and saggy eyelids. They had already drunk a bottle of wine each.

"But why does it matter now?" asked Chloe. "I've called him Grandpa my whole life. No one minded."

Silence hung in the room, and Channing felt everyone's eyes on him. One of the women, Gabriela, retrieved her phone, tapped hastily, and Pavarotti's rich voice filled the room. Perhaps she'd hoped to ease the tension. It didn't help. Everyone returned to their conversations, their voices quiet, faces waxen.

Soon, everyone was invited to take their places at the tables. The children sat at their small table, and the nine adults took their places at the dinner table.

The women were seated at the other end of the table, and Channing sat at Leo's left hand. He wondered if it was because that would be the easiest way for his grandfather to grab a gun to shoot him if the result of the DNA test in a perfectly white envelope lying in front of Leo's empty plate was negative.

One of Joe's four sons, Joseph "Chin," sat to Channing's left, a thin, sad man with almost no chin at all—Channing guessed the nickname was ironic in this case—who looked like an accountant. Finally, there was Albert, a short man who looked like everything pissed him off.

The main entertainment was Albert exchanging loud, angry insults with Fred. Was this some sort of family ritual before they started to talk about something serious?

The parallels in the power structure with the Viking Age were hard to ignore. In his father's mead hall, there was a table of honor for his father, who was the jarl, or earl, and his wife. Guests sat in order of importance at their long tables.

Although they all shared one table, the Esposito family sat just like that. Leo sat at the head of the table. Channing was to his left. Joe sat next to him. One chair, to Leo's right and opposite Channing, was empty. Was this where Daniel usually sat?

Leo Esposito scanned the guests at the table silently, his chest rising and falling quickly. He hadn't drunk a drop of his wine, only turning the glass, red liquid swirling this way and the other. The room was filled with the scents of cured meat, garlic, and olive oil. The family were helping themselves to appetizers: hair-thin carpaccio, serrano, olives glistening in oil.

Channing had taken some bruschetta, with fresh tomatoes and onions, as well as caprese salad that, despite the struggle to get fresh produce, was made with buffalo mozzarella, fresh tomatoes, and basil leaves.

But he couldn't touch the food, and, like his grandfather, he hadn't touched the red wine in his glass. What was the point? Nothing about this evening was worth celebrating or mourning.

He just had to get through it.

He was sure Leo Esposito was his grandfather, unfortunately. But there was always a chance something could go wrong during the DNA test, especially given it had been rushed by Leo's men and their guns. Human error was always a possibility.

Or something else he couldn't control.

Like destiny.

"Will you please just open it?" said Channing quietly, under the roar of Joe's laughter.

Leo threw a long glance at him. "I already know."

Channing leaned back in his chair and took his first sip. The wine went down smooth and rich, and the warmth of alcohol spread through Channing's veins.

Leo took out his gun and laid it on the table with a quiet thud. The guests stopped talking, and only Albert chewed his serrano, watching the gun. Three waiters entered with plates of pasta and pizza, and the only sound in the room for a while was the clanking of the dishes as they put them in front of the guests.

But as the waiters left the room, no one touched their food. From the speakers, Pavarotti sang "O Sole Mio," his effortlessly beautiful voice disturbingly cheerful. One hand still on the gun, Leo reached his other hand into the pocket of his suit and retrieved something. He laid the paper square on the single empty plate to his left, and Daniel's handsome face stared at Channing. Dark-brown hair, green eyes, straight chin, high cheekbones. A small patch of hair that had always stuck out of the sleek business haircut.

"Jesus, Leo," said Joe. "Is it his birthday today? Did I forget?"

"It's not," said Leo. "It's not."

Everyone else kept silent and stared between Leo and Daniel's photo.

"Come on, Leo," said Gabriela, "what is it?"

Leo gave her a long stare. "You all know how I miss him."

The family nodded. "Who do you miss?" asked Chloe.

"Shh," said Matteo. "Grandpa doesn't like to talk about him."

"Not your grandpa," replied Leo tiredly. "And Matteo is

right. I don't like to talk about my son. It hurts too much. You wouldn't remember your uncle Dan, Chloe, you were too little."

He lifted the gun, and everyone at the table shifted away and froze.

"This was his gun," Leo said.

Adrenaline shot through Channing like a burst of fire. His fist clenched around the smooth, carved chair arm.

"He died two years ago." Leo brushed the gun with one thumb and looked at Dan's photo. "But I feel like he's still with us." He lifted the envelope and showed it to everyone. "Because he sent me him." He pointed with the gun at Channing. "This man is our family. This DNA test is positive. He's of my blood."

Channing's heart dropped. Surprised gasps ran around the table. Leo stood up, turned the gun with the handle to Channing, and handed it to him. When Channing took it, Leo pulled him up and hugged him.

"Welcome to the family," Leo said. "I'll tell them you're my son. You can't possibly be my grandson. That's what we'll tell Dan, too, once I go back in time and stop his death."

Channing pulled back from his hug. "But I'm here. You don't need Dan anymore."

Leo chuckled. "Do you think I'll pass up the opportunity to prevent my son's death?"

As Channing's new family members gathered around him, congratulating him, clapping him on the shoulder, kissing him on the cheeks, he watched Leonardo's cool eyes. Dan's gun burned against Channing's hand. He wanted to throw it out of the window and into the ocean and let it sink into the abyss.

"It's good," said Fred as he clapped Channing on the shoulder. "We need help now that we're expanding into gun trafficking."

"Gun trafficking?" Channing's stomach knotted.

"Well, yes," said Leo. "Thanks to you, my boy. When Clicker arranged to smuggle in your nuclear reactor, he opened up a whole new market. Military grade weapons. Explosives. Haven't you heard? The whole world is going down. Everyone needs weapons."

The blood chilled in Channing's veins.

"When is he swearing *omertà*?" asked Joe.

"Tonight," said Leo, turning back to Channing. "After you become a made man, you can deal with Mafia business. I have a sit-down tomorrow with Luca. He's a distributor, and I'm missing a large chunk of money from him." His eyes locked on Channing's. "Prove you really are in the family with your oath. Then get me that money by whatever means necessary."

Meaning, threaten the guy. Perhaps even kill the guy.

Was he capable of that? Killing men in battle, protecting his life and his loved ones was one thing.

Killing in cold blood because someone didn't pay was another.

Could he live with himself? Could he look Ella in the eye after that?

This was all to stop Ragnarök, he reminded himself. But was it worth taking one life to save many others?

To save the chance of his personal happiness?

TWELVE

Something happened.

Ella could feel it as soon as she touched the spindle. The vibration in the air. Her dad's face blurred as though fog descended over it.

Reality slipped. The edge of her ability to stop time was right at her fingertips, invisible, but tangible like a whiff of warm wind. As though the air was denser right next to her hand... She could almost grab it, literally grab it like a thread and attach it to the hook of the spindle, and if she did, she would be able to stop it and spin it back or forward.

But she couldn't quite do it. She tensed, her shoulders aching from strain.

And the more she tensed, the more it slipped away.

Her sinews strained and corded.

And then it was gone.

The blur disappeared. Dad was clear again. Warm yellow light filled the room.

"No!" she growled out.

Dad rolled his chair to her. "What?"

"I had it. I just had it! Goddamn it."

"That's great, isn't it?"

Panting, she brushed sweat off her forehead with the back of her hand.

"Do you want to try again?" Dad asked.

She looked at the spindle in her hand. She was still holding it, and yet, nothing was happening. "I definitely do."

She put the spindle on the table, and it rolled half an inch. How did it work? What had she done exactly? Most importantly, what had she *failed* to do?

Was it just because this spindle was wooden and she needed a golden one? Channing had that meeting today with Leo Esposito to try to get the port back. She hadn't heard anything yet. "Channing, I sure hope you get us access to that golden spindle today..." she muttered. She hoped he wasn't putting himself into even more danger by confronting the Mafia directly, but she had to trust that he knew what he was doing.

She sighed and looked at her dad. Her first attempt with the spindle had left her tired and breathless. But she'd keep trying until she couldn't anymore.

"I want to travel in time," she said and grabbed the spindle.

As her fingers closed around the carved wood, there was an invisible blast of some substance in the air. Dad became blurry again, and she could sense the dense air right next to her hand. She knew if she could just grab it, she would be able to stop it and control it.

But no matter how much she strained, she could move only her physical hand.

And she needed to grasp on to something else...whatever that dense air was. With something that went beyond her physical body.

Sweat covered her back. Her stomach hardened. It was as

though she were pushing against a train. She roared, trying to reach for that something. Seconds ticked past. Time didn't slow. When the pain in her strained muscles became unbearable, she let go.

Right away, everything sharpened around her again. She replaced the spindle on the table and put her hands on her knees, trying to catch her breath.

"Anything?" Dad asked.

"No."

"Okay, time for a break, hon."

Ella paced along the length of the dinner table. "No break. What I don't understand is...in my dreams, it was always effortless. When I was awake and touched that spindle, I wasn't even consciously aware that I was going to do anything... beyond my physical abilities. I didn't do anything at all. Just touched it. And then, when I saved Channing from the protestors and the arrow, I didn't even have a spindle in my hand."

"But this spindle helps?"

"I don't know if it does." She straightened her back and rolled her unbandaged shoulder.

"Why are you sweating?" Dad asked.

"Because I'm trying to reach for something that's unreachable."

"Using your body?"

"Of course. What else?"

"Well...did you use it so much when you traveled in time before?"

"No."

"Then maybe you should try to reach for...whatever it is... without using your physical body."

"Right. Easy for you to say."

"Maybe it's like shooting? You need to keep your body

relaxed, your breath easy and level. Effortless. Keep your eye on the target."

She pinched her shirt at the chest and flapped back and forth to cool herself off. "Okay. Let me try again."

She stood up and picked up the spindle. No blur came, no change in the air. She looked at Dad. "I'm not even sure I need this thing."

"Maybe you don't."

She placed it back on the table, then grabbed it again. "Doesn't feel right. Like I need something to grab on to."

Dad nodded. "Like a gun. Something to shoot with, metaphorically speaking. Makes sense."

"I want to travel in time," she said.

And there it was, that blurring haziness. The something that was at her fingertips. Like Dad suggested, she didn't tense and didn't try to physically grab it. Instead, she breathed and waited. Breathed and waited.

I want to travel in time. I want to travel in time. I want to travel in time.

The more she let go of her physical body, the more reality blurred. The hazier and slower everything became around her.

She was entering a strange dreamlike state, somewhere between being awake and asleep. Like she sometimes did in a dangerous situation.

Until time slowed completely and...stopped.

Dense air was right in her hand, and she could feel it, thin and long, like a thick thread, only invisible.

Nervousness hit her, clenching the muscles in her shoulders. And reality moved again. Sharpened. The clock ticked.

Dad looked at her, wide-eyed.

"Well?" he asked.

She looked at her hand holding the spindle. There was nothing on the hook. "Well, what?"

"What do you mean, well what? What happened?"

"Sorry. I'm just a little dumbstruck. I could reach it. You were right. I needed to stay relaxed and calm. Why?"

"You sort of…"

"What?"

"Started to fade."

Ella looked at the spindle. "Fade?"

"For a moment or two, yes."

She'd faded…almost disappeared…

"I need to try again."

She wasn't sure if saying the words *I want to travel in time* worked, but she wasn't sure what else to try.

She repeated them over and over, still holding the spindle, commanding herself to relax and go into that space where she could feel the dense air and make threads out of time.

But nothing happened.

It was as though she'd spooked the channel, or whatever it was, by being nervous. Like a startled wild animal, it was gone.

Anxiety locked her muscles. What if she'd never be able to access it again?

Ella's shoulders ached from tension. Distantly, she noticed Gloria come home from work and get Ted to bed. Her wound hurt like crazy. Exhaustion weighed on her like a heavy blanket.

The sense of failure settled in the pit of her stomach as she climbed into bed. She checked her phone, but there was nothing from Channing. Where the hell was he? Apart from sending the email about the runes, he hadn't been in touch with her today at all.

She laid her hand on the empty pillow where he'd spent the night after they got back from the past three days ago. Her fingertips brushed the soft, smooth fabric.

She had made some progress today, she supposed. She had

managed to pause time for a moment. She wished she had the power to say "Channing, come back to me," and he'd be right here. Taking her into his arms. Kissing her. Burying his head in her hair.

Only, she wasn't a good Norn, and she wasn't a good witch.

Or Ragnarök would already have stopped.

THIRTEEN

She held Channing's sword in her hands and he knelt in front of her. The sky was black. The earth was on fire. Three Viking ships were docked at the Port of Boston's pier and rocked on the burning sea, their hulls and sails aflame.

It smelled like burning flesh and hair and wood. It smelled like blood and hot iron. Wolves fought with people...the police...the FBI...the Vikings. The Mafia fired their guns at everyone.

And she knew this was the end.

"Stand up!" she yelled at him. "Stand up!"

Strong arms wrapped around her waist, and her back was pressed against a hard torso.

The vision was gone, and she relaxed. Just a stupid dream.

"Hmmmmm," he moaned, burying his face in the crease between her shoulder and her neck.

"I did manifest you after all, didn't I...?" Without opening her eyes, she wriggled tighter into his embrace. She pushed her butt into his crotch and felt his erection press against her beneath the fabric of his trousers.

"And you feel so good," she mumbled.

Stirring her sleepy, heavy body into something fiery and hot, he ran his hand under the loose T-shirt she'd worn to bed, up her stomach, and cupped one breast. She gasped as pleasure spilled through her like warm honey. As he started teasing her nipple, she bit her lip and arched her back, making a circular motion against his erection with her butt.

"Ah, woman," he growled. "Don't tease me. I don't want your father to have to kill me."

"He won't," she whispered and giggled. "We're like teenagers..."

He nuzzled her neck, pressing her harder into his body. "I certainly want you like I'm a horny fourteen-year-old."

Her insides clenched, a sweet burn of desire building between her legs. "So don't fight this," she whispered. "I want you, too."

She'd never been a seductress, never initiated sex. She'd also never wanted anyone like she wanted him.

With him, sex was better every time. What would it be like to have a lifetime of this? A lifetime where they'd know each other's bodies, know how to please each other, how to bring each other to the sweetest pleasure...

He turned her head to him and took her mouth. His kiss tasted of hunger and need, and she melted against him. With his fingers gently pulling, playing, massaging her breasts, and his other arm around her like an iron band, and his mouth on hers, she was dissolving.

"What do you want, Ella?" he growled against her mouth.

In response, with her healthy arm, she reached back until she touched his belt and unbuckled it.

"You," she whispered.

"You have me already. You always will."

Heat pulsed between her legs, and her heart drummed in

her chest. She was opening up to him. She already had, but with every word, with every touch, she was giving in, surrendering to him completely.

Believing he was hers. And if he was hers, she could trust him like she could trust no one else in the world.

She could actually have this happiness that so many women in the world had—she could have it, too.

She already had it.

She felt him push his trousers and his briefs down his legs, and his hot erection dug into her hip.

"Your shirt, too," she whispered, barely managing to form the words.

She felt him shift away and move, and when he came back to her, his hard chest and stomach were like a hot, velvety stone against her.

"Your panties," he said, his voice urgent and rough.

She looked back at him. His eyes were dark and needy and a little frightening, like the eyes of a wild wolf. Her pulse pounded painfully. "What about them?" she whispered innocently, digging her butt cheeks into his crotch.

His breathing changed. His chest rose and felt quickly against her back, his eyes dark. A slow smile spread on his lips. "Playing with me, sweetheart?"

"You like it," she said, not a question. A statement.

He liked it because he was a warrior. He liked it because he was a conqueror. He liked it because she defied him. Because she was a challenge.

Instead of responding, he slid his hands down. Something tore and snapped, and her hips were completely naked.

She gasped, and the slight sting of the torn elastic resonated right through into her sex, making her throb. He gripped her uppermost leg and lifted it. His other hand went between her legs. He spread her open with his thumb and index finger and rubbed her, sending pleasure rippling through her.

"Fuck, you're so wet," he whispered.

She moaned, feeling her eyes roll back.

Then he let her go, rolled onto his back, and Ella heard a rip of plastic. In a moment, he was back to her. He lifted her leg up again, and his cock was nudging against her.

She was pounding with white-hot need, and when he slid inside her, she whimpered from the fullness and the pleasure and the connection with him. Sweet, hot bliss blossomed through her body as he began sliding in and out. He was completely pressed against her, spooning her, and one hand was on her clit and rubbing it.

She was trembling all over, blind from desire. She felt impossibly full with his big, hard cock pounding in and out of her, his hand stroking and pinching her clit, and the feel of him, the scent of him—all masculine musk and expensive cologne and fresh sweat and sex—and this soul-deep, out-of-this-world connection. This feeling like she'd touched the divine. Like she'd found her peace.

Like she was whole.

The orgasm slammed through her like a tsunami. Her mind was chaos and emptiness, explosions of sweetness rocking her like waves in a storm.

When she was still, they both breathed raggedly. His arms were like two iron rods around her, his face buried in her hair.

"I love you, Ella," he murmured. "You are everything."

"You, too," she echoed back, wrapping her arms around his.

After a while, her mind cleared, and she turned to him. "How was your day? Where were you? I haven't heard from you since you sent the information about the runes."

His handsome face darkened, his eyes hard on the ceiling. "Don't ask."

"Did you meet with Leo Esposito?"

"Yes."

"And? What about the time machine spindle?"

"We don't have the spindle yet."

"What happened?"

Something dark and stubborn flashed in his eyes and he didn't reply. Instead, he leaned down and kissed her, shutting her up. But she pushed against him and looked at him. "No, no, you won't distract me with your kisses and your perfect hard body this time."

She sat up in bed.

"What the hell happened with the Mafia?"

He lay back on the pillow and put his hands behind his head.

"Channing!"

"Ella—"

She pulled her T-shirt on, left the safe warmth of the bed, and began pacing her room, wooden planks screeching as she stepped on them. "What the fuck! Why won't you tell me? You know you're making it worse, right?"

"Lower your voice. You'll wake up your family."

"Are you kidding me? You were with the Mafia, in real danger, and you're not telling me anything, and I'm supposed to keep quiet?"

He stood up, still naked, and pulled her into his embrace. His scent melted into her bones. "I was with them only for a short time."

She resisted his pull, shaking her head and pushing hard against him. "And?"

His face fell, and he turned away from her. "It's complicated. I also spent a lot of time with Giana, trying to sort out the legal stuff around my arrest and my charges. The police are so much slower now and the courts basically don't function, so for now I'm not their main headache. So we're trying to get the Mafia out of the port using the legal route."

She cupped his face and turned him to look into her eyes. "The legal route? When the courthouses are not working? You're not serious. What are you not telling me?"

He picked up his briefs and put them on. "It's better for you if you don't know everything."

There was such a vulnerability in his voice, an edge of something broken, something fragile.

"You're kidding me, right? I spent tonight trying to activate my powers. It would help me to know if that giant golden spindle works or not. I thought we were a team."

He ran his hand through his hair. "We are a team."

She took his face in her hands. "Good. So tell me the truth."

He kissed the palm that cupped his face and said nothing.

She pressed. "We're in this together, right? Don't you dare hide stuff from me. Remember what happened when you didn't tell me about the time machine?"

"A disaster."

"A disaster. So?"

She saw the moment he almost told her, the moment he opened his mouth…

But it passed, and he lowered his head and shook it. "The less you know, the better. And they can't suspect you and I are together. I won't put your family at risk."

"It's just a matter of time before they find out. The Mafia knows the cop families."

He stepped away from her and put on his suit pants. "Exactly. It's just a matter of time, and I'd like to use the time we have. I'm going home. Will you come with me?"

She shook her head, helplessness weighing at her. How could she reach for him when he didn't want to open up to her?

"No. I have to get up early for a shift."

He put on his dress shirt and then buttoned it, his eyes dark and impassive on her. "What happened with your powers?"

She shook her head. "Not much. There was some progress, I suppose. Dad, Rob, and Ted made a wooden spindle, and it worked a bit...but I think the golden spindle is the answer."

She felt the distance between them like an icy vastness. After the soul-deep connection of their lovemaking, it chilled her.

This was new. They'd argued before. They'd hated each other in the beginning—or at least she had hated him.

But this... Even when they'd argued in the hut, she hadn't felt locked out of his thoughts and feelings.

He was hiding something from her. She could almost smell it.

As though hearing her thoughts, he covered the distance between them and towered over her.

"Come with me. Let's forget about everything. Just be you and me and nothing else. I need you. I need to feel you. I need to know you're still mine."

She looked up at him. "Of course I'm still yours. Why wouldn't I be?"

Sadness filled his eyes. "You might not be if you knew everything."

"You told me your loyalty was to me."

He kissed her forehead. "Remember that. Please, remember that."

The next moment, he was gone.

FOURTEEN

The next day, the police station was even more chaotic. The holding cells were so full, the cops had to make judgment calls. Less severe offenders got fines and warnings and were released. Those who were charged with murder, rape, burglary, and other serious offenses were added to the overflowing holding cells.

By lunchtime, Ella's head pounded. The noise of people talking and phones ringing in the office was deafening. The room smelled of wet clothes and body odor. Dirty puddles of melted snow collected here and there, and the floor was filthy. Ella rubbed her forehead, staring at but not seeing the computer screen before her.

She took a painkiller and washed it down with instant coffee in a plastic cup. It tasted bitter and chemical, and she winced.

Her talk with Channing yesterday worried her. It wasn't just that he wouldn't tell her what had happened with the Mafia, it was the look in his eyes. Like whatever had happened, it was bad. And the distance between them knotted her stomach.

She was about to stand up and get the next offender to process their case when Ricardo marched into the office, his normally relaxed face a pale mask. He was putting on his jacket and looking at her.

"What?" she asked.

He walked to her. "That arsonist Gleeson just gave me a tip about Surtr Enterprises," he said quietly.

Her stomach dropped. "What tip?"

"A big gun-running deal is happening today. He gave me the address in Quincy."

"Oh, shit." Ella put on her jacket and checked her gun. "How sure are we that this is legit?"

"Not sure at all. I don't have any proof. So I can't go to Wilson."

"Okay, but I'm coming with you."

He looked around. "Wilson said he needs as many cops as possible processing cases."

"I know. But this is gun running. If we don't bust them, there may be a whole shipment of unregistered weapons on the streets. That won't do anything to help our caseload."

"Okay. Let's go."

Besides what she'd said to Ricardo, Ella was sure Surtr Enterprises had some connection to Ragnarök. That name couldn't just be a coincidence.

But when they reached the station parking lot, Ricardo's phone rang, and he grabbed it. His face lost all color. "*Ya voy*," he said and hung up.

"I have to go, Ella. My sister just called me... Wolves are attacking people in my neighborhood."

"Oh. I'll come with you."

"No. Someone needs to check on Surtr, gather evidence to stop whatever shit they're up to. Can you go there?"

"Yes, of course, but are you sure you don't want my help?"

He was already in the driver's seat. "I'm sure. Just be careful."

He closed the door and drove away.

The address led her to an industrial area of Quincy, a southern suburb of Boston. The warehouse was abandoned and neglected. Parts of the walls were missing, and rebar stuck out of the corroded concrete like spider legs reaching out in search of someone. How could this be the address of a working company? Maybe this was just where the deal was going down.

She parked in the lot along the wall of the warehouse, pulling in behind what must have once been a decorative bush, now growing out of control. The parking lot held several corroding cars with smashed windows. This was a good enough spot to blend in. The bush provided enough cover to allow her to duck in case someone looked her way.

She didn't have to wait long. Through the naked branches, she saw three black SUVs driving up to the building, snow flying from under their tires. The first SUV stopped, and men in suits leaped out of it. Leonardo Esposito was one of them.

After him, holding a gun, came Channing.

FIFTEEN

Inside, the abandoned warehouse was quiet.

It had snowed even more yesterday. Earlier this morning, the made men had arrived to pick Channing up in cars with chains on the wheels, cutting through the snow with no problem.

And, of course, they had no problem with fuel. Every gas station would serve them first, while the rest of the population had to suffer.

While the Mafia was riding around in style, making the world a worse place, hospitals couldn't send ambulances to pick up the sick and wounded. Trucks couldn't deliver much-needed food.

Channing had been astonished to see several people riding horses in Boston and even a few horse-drawn sleighs being driven through the city streets.

The interior walls of the warehouse were covered with rust and dirt stains. Daylight fell through the giant opening at the front, which was covered with black soot. It looked like an explosion had torn up the front corner of the building, and rebar stuck out of the ragged wound. Right at the edge of the black spot, the word *Surtr* was visible, dark red and faded like an old bloodstain.

Snowdrifts had gathered at the entrance, but this deep in the building, the cement floor was clear. Chipped yellow stripes delineated walking paths that no one would ever take again. A pile of industrial shelving with broken boards lay in a dark corner. Chains hanging from the metal beams swung from the slight icy wind and screeched.

The smell of iron reminded him of blood. Of every battle he'd fought in the Viking Age.

Leo stood behind Channing, and Channing felt his estimating gaze like fireplace pokers. Behind them, stood more made men and goons. All armed. All waiting.

Soon, the whisper of car tires sounded from outside, and then several male silhouettes filled the entrance. Shoes rustled and clunked as the men walked to the center of the warehouse.

In front of the procession was Luca Bertino, a surprisingly big and muscular man for a drug runner. Though, recently he'd become a gun runner, Channing reminded himself.

He was bald, and one of his ears was pierced. A tattoo of an angel, wings spread, covered his left cheek and the back of his head.

Behind him, stood three men in a formation that gave Channing the immediate impression of a *skjaldborg*, a shield wall. But he didn't pay a lot of attention to them; his focus was on Luca.

Channing turned to Leo and murmured, "Couldn't you pick a less memorable guy for the job? Bet he's on every police report ever filed."

Leo shrugged. "Shut up. He's a capo, as loyal as a dog."

Capo was a medium rank in the Mafia. Made man was the lowest. Channing had become a made man yesterday after dinner. He now was a fully initiated member of the Mafia. He fit the bill—was of Italian descent and sponsored not just by a Mafia man, but by the boss himself.

The clicking of a grenade sounded next to Leo. "Wouldn't you know it, the made man."

Clicker was a tall man in a beanie and a leather jacket. Not like a Mafia man at all. They were all in business suits and had clean haircuts. This man was wild. Several weeks ago, he'd made the arrangements for Channing to get his nuclear reactor.

Channing gave him a sour look.

Standing now with Dan Esposito's gun in his hand, with a dozen armed goons and made men in expensive suits, he felt powerful. He felt the strength of the brotherhood.

A brotherhood he'd been sworn into by a blood oath.

He'd taken the oath of *omertà*, the Mafia code of silence. It meant he couldn't talk to the authorities, couldn't betray the Mafia.

Or he'd be dead.

And he couldn't even share it with Ella. Not for his sake— for hers. For her safety.

Once, in the ninth century, he'd sworn an oath to his father, the Viking jarl. That had been when he was a teenager and had thought his life would be dedicated to serving his father and then becoming the jarl himself.

Then he'd sworn an oath to Ella, the woman he loved.

The woman he wanted to make his wife.

Swearing an oath of loyalty to the Mafia was the third one. And since he was a man of his word, it would be very hard to break it. Even if it was a horrible oath.

But he would have to break it one day. Because he'd given it for *her*. He'd given it for a chance of *them*.

And he'd need to stay alive, somehow.

"I am a made man," he said. "And I don't need to have been

in the Mafia for years to know Luca isn't as loyal as a dog. Or we wouldn't be having this meeting."

Leo cocked one eyebrow and hid a smile, then stepped back.

Channing sighed and studied Luca, who stood looking at him calmly, his back straight, hands clasped. As odd as this meeting was, with so many men holding guns, and in this snowed-in, decrepit warehouse, this was like a CEO meeting with an employee who was neglecting his responsibilities. This was business management. And he'd had plenty of those kinds of meetings.

"Well, Luca," Channing said and tucked Dan's gun at the back of his suit trousers. "You owe the family two hundred thousand dollars, don't you?"

Luca nodded, not changing his expression. "Yes. The last batch of ATI GSGs sold out like hotcakes. Surtr did well by starting the production of those German rifles here in Boston."

Channing walked closer to him. "So." He stopped about one step away from Luca, staring him straight in his eyes. "Where's the money?"

Luca shrugged. "No money."

He appeared cool and collected, almost indifferent, with his straight shoulders, his feet set wide apart. But the vein on his smooth temple beat quickly, his eyes were just a tad too wide, and he was swaying slightly from side to side. He was nervous. He was ready to flee. Despite the fact that he'd been patted all over for guns, Channing couldn't help wondering if he had something hidden somewhere. His index finger was tapping against the back of his hand, perhaps itching to take out the weapon and defend himself.

Channing chuckled. "You don't have the money. Okay. Where is it then?"

Luca looked at Leo. "I don't have it, boss. My distributors didn't give me the profits. God's truth."

Of course, Channing wasn't an authority here yet. He was seeing Luca for the first time in his life, whereas Leo was Luca's leader.

"You're lying," Channing said, and Luca looked back at him, a frown of anger flashing across his face. He wasn't afraid of Channing, he was afraid of Leo.

"I'm not lying. Who the fuck are you, and why the fuck should I report anything to you?"

Behind Channing, Leo chuckled. "Excellent question. What do you say to it, Channing Hakonson?"

Channing cursed. He knew this was a system based on power. In the Viking world, Channing's father had inherited the title of jarl from his own father, but his men respected him because he was one of the best warriors they knew. Because he was powerful and just, and he protected his people. He was a man of honor.

In a perverse way, the same hierarchy applied here. Power and the strength of one's word meant everything, although these principles were tainted by crime. These people served the wrong business model. But they were still warriors, and they followed a code of conduct like any military or police organization.

Channing had to show them he was one of them.

"I may be new here," he said, "but that doesn't mean I'm going to be fooled." He turned to one of the goons who'd driven him here. "Ottavio, bring my case from the trunk."

The goon nodded and went to the car.

Channing turned to Luca. "You're lying because you've pretty much told me you are. I know men like you. I have fired several of you over the years." He nodded back at the crumbled wall of the warehouse. "The world is sinking into chaos, and you think you can get away with it." He looked at Luca again. "But you can't. I won't let you."

He felt someone staring at him like he was under a microscope. His eyes drifted to the men behind Luca.

And when his gaze stopped at a familiar face, he froze. At first, shock didn't let him fully understand who it was. Tall, handsome face, high cheekbones, pale-green eyes.

Nick Murphy.

Ella's ex.

An Irish mobster.

Channing hadn't been involved with the Mafia long to know the politics of the criminal organizations, but he was pretty sure the Irish mob wasn't supposed to be involved with Luca. Nick watched him without blinking, like a wild animal, tracking his every movement. Nick's chest rose and fell quickly under the expensive suit. He was clean-shaven and had gotten a haircut. No one would ever know he wasn't Mafia.

Channing looked at the other two men behind Luca. Nothing special about them. One was a bit older, bigger, and rounder, the other a bit taller and scrawnier. Both wore suits and looked well groomed. Were they in the Irish mob, too?

Why were they here?

He didn't like this at all.

Especially because Nick knew exactly who Channing had been with the other day. If Nick decided to tell them he'd seen Channing with a cop, Channing would be dead.

So would Ella and her family.

Icy tension crushed his gut. Sweat covered his back.

They stared at each other. They both knew who the other was. Neither of them was supposed to be here.

And if either of them betrayed their information, they would be dead.

Tension crackled in the air like that ice sheet on the frozen lake just before he had fallen through it.

"I know you're lying, Luca," Channing said slowly. "You are betraying the Mafia. And you know better than me what happens to traitors."

Nick's hand next to his belt twitched, no doubt a reflex to grab his gun. Luca blinked and fidgeted. The power pose, the protective pose, was broken. Instead, he went on the attack and stabbed his finger into Channing's face.

"You have no idea what you're talking about. You're no one! Why should anyone listen to you?"

Ottavio stood next to Channing with his case. Channing asked him to open it, and in the white-gray light of the concrete building, his sword glistened sharply. Channing lifted it.

The weight of it, the feel of the antler handle under his fingers, the gorgeous Viking patterns interweaving, playing together, brought something back into him. The power. The strength. The anger, almost holy.

This guy was leading them all into a trap. Channing had already had this happen several times. His father had dealt with this, too, but back in the Viking Age, he'd made the traitors outlaws. He didn't kill them like other Viking jarls did. He'd send them away and pronounce them outside the law.

In the Viking Age, it meant they were worse than slaves. Anyone could do anything to an outlaw. Anyone could kill them or enslave them without fear of punishment. They would be declined food and shelter in villages, no one would talk to them, no one would trade with them.

"What the fuck is that?" Luca said, taking a step back.

Channing pointed his sword at him. "Are you lying to the boss, Luca?"

"No."

"Tell me one thing. I'm new here, right? What's the punishment for a lie?"

Luca swallowed. "Finger cut off."

Channing cursed inwardly. He really didn't want to mutilate anyone. He also didn't want to kill. He clenched his teeth. How far would he go to stop Ragnarök?

Luca's eyes widened, and he took another step back, paling, and Nick and the other two behind him exchanged quick, worried glances, their hands stiff, ready to grab their guns.

Someone would die today. The Irish mob and the Mafia were the biggest competitors in the Boston underworld. If Luca had brought mobsters to a meeting like this today, this was a hostile takeover.

They had come to obliterate the Mafia. To kill the don.

He had no proof, just his instinct.

He pointed his sword at the man's hand, and one of his men grabbed Luca's hand and pressed it against a crate. "Great. So who bought the ATI GSGs? Surely you can tell us that."

Channing brought the sword closer to Luca's hand. "I don't know. People. Street gangs. Europe. Everybody wanted them."

"Europe. Germany produces them, so I'm guessing it's not too difficult to get a hold of them there. So why would they buy from the States? All that effort to get them shipped across the ocean."

"Surtr's production costs are low, but the quality is the same."

"Hmm... Good times for the gun trade. What part of Europe?"

Despite the cold, a drop of sweat formed on Luca's forehead.

"What part of Europe, Luca?" Channing said slowly, calmly as he pressed the edge of his sword against the man's finger.

Luca swallowed and his eyes darted to his side just for a split moment. To where Nick stood.

Nick's frown intensified, his face as stiff as a mask.

Channing pressed harder, and a small drop of blood formed at the edge of the blade.

"Ireland," Luca moaned out.

Channing was right. He'd hit the bull's-eye. The Mafia wouldn't sell the guns to Ireland. It was the Irish mob. Luca was going to kill his own.

Brothers killing brothers...

Even within the mob, the ties of kinship didn't mean anything.

He would kill the Mafia boss and maintain the business relationship with Surtr Enterprises, only supplying the world with the guns through the mob connections. When better to take a chance than right when the world was ending, anyway? Channing wondered if the rest of the family had been targeted, too.

Slowly, Channing turned his head back and looked at Leonardo, and mouthed one word. *Hide.*

Leo's frown straightened in realization. Bullets rained down on them from behind the crates, the walls, but instead of ducking and hiding, Leo darted forward and pulled Channing by the collar to hide behind a turned-over truck.

They leaned with their backs against the truck. Channing panted. His sword was useless against bullets. As bullets ricocheted around them, Leo pulled out his gun and peered from behind the crate.

His grandfather might have just saved his life.

"You okay?" Channing asked, looking him over.

Leo aimed and fired. "I'm fine."

Three of Leo's men had been shot, now lying in pools of

blood. Ottavio was one of them. That could have been Channing if it wasn't for Leo.

For a split second, he imagined what it would be like to have family here. What he'd seen at the dinner yesterday wasn't what he'd imagined the Mafia to be like. It was about family. Kids. Shared meals. Talking about your day.

"The mob," Channing panted. "One of the men that was with Luca is from the Irish mob. They were going to obliterate us. They must have had men waiting to ambush us. The bastards hid men in the warehouse before we arrived."

Leo's eyes widened. "Fuck. Then it makes sense they sold the guns to Ireland. But how did you know?"

"I saw the guy not long ago robbing people of groceries and overheard him bragging about the mob."

Leo's men were hiding behind shelves, abandoned machine equipment, crates and cars, shooting at the heads flickering between the crates by the exit. There might have been more of the enemy outside the building. Leo was, however, aiming in the direction of Luca.

"Cover me," said Leo. "I'm going to take out the fucking traitors."

He crawled from behind their shelter, but Channing pulled him back by his coat. "Hell no."

"What do you mean, hell no? Just shoot at him. Cover me!"

It would have been so much easier to let Leo go into the danger of the open space where any bullet could take him. Then he wouldn't need to worry about his grandfather traveling in time to save Dan. He would be able to destroy the time machine so much more easily. Without Leo Esposito, the world would probably be a better place.

But he couldn't let him do that. Maybe he wasn't the most humane, but Leo was still his grandfather...the only grandfather he'd ever known.

"No. Stay right here. This is suicide."

Leo's green eyes warmed, and a small smile touched his face. "This is just like with Dan. I'd be having the same conversation with him." He clapped Channing on the cheek. "My boy. You are family now."

With an excited roar, he patted Channing on the shoulder, grinning. Despite Channing's protest, he crawled out from behind the truck and, surprisingly quickly for his age, sprinted across the empty space of the warehouse. He hid behind a stack of metal sheets, and several bullets ricocheted off the metal right where his head was.

The next moment, he peeked from behind the sheets, aimed, and shot. Nick fell from behind a container and didn't move. Blood pooled around his head.

Luca's goons saw him and ran. Leo's men followed them. When no more sounds of shooting came, Leo came out of his shelter and approached Channing, who stood up. "Nice work, my boy. Even Dan wouldn't have been able to tell that this piece of shit betrayed us. Come." He hugged Channing around the shoulder, and they walked towards the exit. "Nice trick with the sword, by the way. But don't bring it again. You're in the family now. Italian. Right?"

Channing gritted his teeth. "Right."

"Okay. We'll have dinner, and I'll show you the books. You'll tell me what you think. You're an excellent businessman. You have it from me, no doubt. Now, with you by my side, we'll build an incredible business."

A business that sold illegal guns and drugs to a world that was already on the brink...

As they walked and Leo kept talking, bile rose in Channing's stomach. He felt dirtier and dirtier. Even though he hadn't killed anyone and had cut off no fingers today, it would only be a matter of time until he would have to.

SIXTEEN

Ella clenched the wheel. Men shot at each other. Bullets pinged off the concrete.

Men fell.

Men died.

Blood bloomed on the snowdrifts, on the tire marks left by the trucks and SUVs that had arrived at the warehouse earlier. One of the men who had appeared in the second group of vehicles was Nick.

Nick and Channing were inside the warehouse. Along with dozens of men with guns, and all she could do was sit and hide and hope no one would see her. She considered calling for backup, but she hoped Channing could negotiate peace between them... If the police came, there would definitely be shooting. And Channing would be in the middle of it.

She considered pulling her gun out and ambushing them, arresting them, doing something... But that would be stupid. Nick's men were probably from the Irish mob.

She'd be alone against them all.

Well, not all of them. Channing would be on her side...

Right?

She had to do everything in her power to spare Channing. To protect him.

And seeing her in danger, who knew what he'd do? He might get himself killed.

And so, like an idiot, she'd waited. It didn't take long, five or ten minutes, before the shooting started. First, shots came from inside.

Then she saw men crawling from another parking lot with guns drawn. Ten...twenty or so of them. They hid behind the soot-black broken walls of the warehouse, staying low, went inside, and shot.

And shot.

And shot.

And she sat helplessly, making herself hide, when all her instincts were to run inside and protect her man. Her heart raced. Adrenaline covered her skin with sweat.

Then the newcomers were running away, and some were shot. They fell.

They died.

Was Channing among them? She was shaking, staring at them so hard her eyes hurt.

Then it was quiet. So quiet, she could hear her heart drum in her ears. A wild, unhealthy gallop. Her palms holding her gun were sweaty; her fingers hurt from holding it so tightly.

Then the Mafia men were walking out of the building. Some of them were wounded. Others carried dead bodies.

She recognized one of the bodies...

It was Nick Murphy. Shock washed over her, even though she had known this could have happened.

Then, holding his sword, Channing walked out next to Leo Esposito, who held a gun.

Their heads leaned together as they talked. Leo gesticulated—enthusiastically. They looked like two bosses discussing an important new deal.

Something flashed in Channing's other hand...

A gun!

Oh, God, had *he* killed Nick?

The thought was like a bomb exploding in her mind.

He had been jealous. He had threatened to kill Nick.

He had met with the Mafia but wouldn't tell her what had happened. That dark, haunted, secretive look...

He'd *betrayed* her. Her mind was chaos, shattered like glass.

What about his oath to her? What about him saying he *loved* her? Did he lie about that, too? What about all his promises to do anything for them?

Was that a lie?

Was Ragnarök making him a monster? A murderer, a Mafia man...

"Goddamn you, Channing," Ella muttered. "What did you do?"

Her phone rang. The ringtone was like the blast of a siren.

"Fuck!"

She shoved her gun into the holster under her blazer, her hands shaking. Her palms were so sweaty, she couldn't get to her phone, which was in her pocket, and it kept blaring and blaring and blaring. *Please, let them not hear it, let them not hear it.*

She glanced up at them as she kept digging. They hadn't heard it yet.

She twisted hard and finally reached it...but her elbow brushed against the horn and the car honked.

With the phone in her hand, she froze and switched off the sound.

She looked up.

Channing, Leo Esposito, and twenty or so Mafia men were staring at her.

"AND WHO THE fuck is that? Can't be the police, they don't dare show up here..." Esposito murmured. "One of Luis's? A woman?" He pulled out his gun and raised it slightly. "Hey, Angelo, take the boys. Check that car out."

As four goons all pulled out their guns, an abyss was spreading under Channing's feet.

Not now. Not now, goddamn it!

Panic gripped him and he shoved it down, commanding himself to get it together and think.

He had to keep them away from her. He needed her to leave.

"No!" He waved with Daniel Esposito's gun. "Stay back. Let me go and check."

"Stay back?" Leo frowned. "What is this? You don't have to be a hero. We have an army to protect you. Come on, guys. Go."

Fucking hell. The men pulled out their guns and walked towards Ella.

Channing hurried and stood before them, blocking their way. "I said no."

Leo's teeth glinted as he bared them. "You don't say no to *my* orders. And you don't fool me. Let's go, Angelo."

He marched past Channing, shoving him in the shoulder. He raised his gun and pointed it straight at Ella. Channing chased him and stood between Leo and Ella. He must be losing his mind.

I'll do anything to stop Ragnarök... I'll do anything for a chance of us...

His promise crawled under his skin, spilling a feverish ache into his muscles.

Anything...

Leo's snarl fell, he paled, and a muscle under his eye twitched. "Get out of my way."

"This may be dangerous *for you*," Channing said.

The car door behind him opened and closed and snow crunched rhythmically as Ella walked towards them.

No.

His anger gone, Leo was watching her from behind Channing with curiosity.

Channing closed his eyes for a moment and let his chin fall onto his chest. He needed to calm down and be on top of his game. He had to protect her, no matter what. If Leo found out that she was a cop... They'd kill Channing and then they'd kill her.

And her family.

He turned to her. She was beaming the brightest smile. Her blond hair was tied into a knot behind her head.

"Hi there!" She waved her hand. "Sorry to butt in on you like that."

Leo and his goons watched her with glossed-over eyes. She wove her fingers into Channing's, connecting their hands, and planted a kiss on his cheek.

"I'm Ella. Channing's fiancée."

No!

Leo's eyebrows crawled up to his hairline. "Fiancée, huh? Well. It's a pleasure. I'm Leo." He put his gun away and stretched his hand out to her, flashing a charming smile. "Channing's father."

Fucking hell!

Ella's eyebrows crawled up to her hairline as she grasped

his hand and shook it in return automatically. She blinked and shot a glance at Channing, a glance full of daggers. She might think this was just a cover he'd come up with. What would she think if he told her this was the truth? That he was Mafia by blood.

"Nice to meet you. Sorry. I was worried about him and was looking for him."

"How did you find him?" asked Leo.

She snorted and grimaced, then pushed Channing's chest playfully. "Ah, you know, a woman never gives away her secrets."

Leo smiled. "See, sweetheart, in this case you better. It being a matter of security and all. No one was supposed to know about this meeting."

She cleared her throat nervously and looked at her shoes. "Um. Yes. Well..." She glanced at Channing from under her brows and pressed her lips together, then leaned towards Leo and lowered her voice. "See, sometimes I worry he cheats on me... And there's this app, FindYourHusband. He didn't know, and now you kinda blew my cover...so..."

Channing suppressed a curse. He hadn't known she could playact like that. This woman was a godsend.

Leo's mouth spread in a crooked smile. "Well, you're almost family now, aren't you? Why do you seem so familiar? Have I seen you somewhere?"

Of course he'd seen her—she'd been among the police that had raided the port to arrest Channing. She had been shooting at Leo's people who'd been there to collect the drugs they'd smuggled inside the nuclear reactor.

"Ah, probably when I visited Channing at his office." She wrapped both her arms around Channing's and laid her head on his shoulder for a moment.

Leo frowned, thinking. "Must be. Well, Channing, you have a beautiful fiancée. I wish you had told me about her. Come, Ella, we must get to know each other better. Let us finish our business and you can wait in the car. I want to welcome you into the family and get to know everything about you."

SEVENTEEN

"What the hell were you thinking?" growled Channing under his breath.

Ella looked at the heads of the two goons in the front seats. Neither of them moved or gave any indication they'd heard Channing. Leo was in the car behind them.

Driving through the snowed-in streets was slow even with chains on the tires, and the houses of Dorchester crawled by through the window. Only five blocks to their right was Ripley Street and her home.

This was not the time or place to get into this, but anger boiled in the pit of her stomach. Hurt from Channing's deception scraped at her insides. The hole within her was aching, gaping, and tearing.

She was alone. Again. Left behind. Abandoned.

He wasn't her home after all.

She couldn't talk about this now. She wouldn't. She was smarter than this.

"You lied to me." The words flew out of her mouth before she could stop them. "You betrayed me."

One of the goons threw a sharp glance at her in the rearview mirror, and she bit her tongue.

"Did you kill him?" she whispered.

Channing didn't look at her. His jaw worked, his profile a stony mask. Twenty feet in front of them, three wolves crossed the street. One of them was holding something wrapped in a bloody cloth in its jaws. They stopped for a moment, looking at the SUV, ears at attention, then calmly sprinted away.

Wolves, never seen in the city before Channing had built the time machine, behaved more and more like Boston was the wilderness. Like they ran through the woods rather than between houses.

"Fucking wolves," muttered one of the goons. "Great hunting season, though. They were sniffing around my house, and I shot them from the porch last night with my brother. Then I shot my brother because he took the wolf I killed."

The goons guffawed, and the back of Ella's neck prickled.

Brothers killing brothers. Here we go again.

"Wolves everywhere, man," said the one who drove. "My cousin in Italy said they got them, too."

"The whole goddamn world needs guns," said the first one darkly. "Soon, people will start hunting each other. Wars everywhere."

"What wars?" asked Channing.

The goon looked at Channing in the mirror. "Where do you live, in a cave? Haven't you seen the news?"

Ella's stomach tightened. She'd been so exhausted last night, she crashed without looking at her phone.

"No," said Channing.

He was probably too preoccupied with whatever dirty business he was doing with Leo Esposito to pay attention to world events.

"A war just broke out between North Korea and China.

Nine ships went out tonight. Full of weapons and explosives from Surtr Enterprises. Three more went out to South Africa—the guns will be transported to other African countries from there. They all steal what's left of their food supplies and then blame each other for sicknesses and for hunger. Two went down to Brazil. The rest to Russia. Kazakhstan attacked the Russian border."

Ella gulped. She was so busy trying to deal with crime in the city, she hadn't paid enough attention to what was happening in the rest of the world. So Surtr *was* involved in the gun trade...and on such a huge scale...

Channing's whole body tightened next to her, and he looked back at Leo's SUV. "How long until we arrive?"

"With this weather...half an hour?"

Ella glanced at her phone, which was still on silent. The call that had outed her to the Mafia had been from the police station. How was Ricardo? Was it him who'd called, or did someone else wonder where she'd gone? God, if they found out about Channing being in the Mafia...about her continued involvement with him...

She switched her phone off completely.

"Half an hour to Cape Cod?" Channing said. "That can't be right."

"Not to Cape Cod."

The fist on Channing's lap clenched even tighter. "Where the fuck are we going?"

"Back Bay. Daniel's house."

Channing whitened.

Daniel...

Who was that? Someone from the Esposito family?

Her mind raced for a moment, and then she knew. The infamous former Boston Mafia boss, the one who was murdered with a sword two years ago on his yacht in the marina.

With a *sword*, not a gun or a knife...

Daniel was Leo's son, and so then he must be Channing's brother...

She looked at Channing, and he met her gaze. "Is Leo really your father?" she whispered.

Channing's eyes were hard and dark on her.

"Dan was my father, Ella," he murmured, his eyes never leaving her. "And Leo is my grandfather."

She sucked in air that didn't seem to fill her lungs.

It seemed, right at the end of the world, that both she and Channing would find their roots.

Hers lay with one of the most powerful beings in the world, a Norn.

His lay with one of the most powerful men in Boston, a Mafia boss.

CHANNING STOOD between Ella and Leo, goons on all sides. The screech of the cast-iron gate opening before them was like a saw against his nerves. Behind the fence, across the snowed-in garden, old footsteps led down the straight path towards a darkened brownstone mansion. Commonwealth Avenue in Back Bay, normally alive with cars passing, pedestrians and people walking their dogs, was desolate.

Formerly majestic, the rows of three-story brownstones now had broken bay windows. Grand entry stairs led to burned or broken-in front doors. Between the front porches, homeless people burned fires from the expensive furniture inside the houses. Most who could afford to leave the city had fled to their summer homes.

Dan's mansion was an exception. A statement. As crime boss, he didn't belong to the upper class of Boston, on the elite street where every house had a history. But that was where, Channing had no doubt, his narcissistic father had chosen to show that he didn't need to be among Boston's elite to be better than everyone else.

By Odin, was this where his mother had been kept captive? Was this where Dan had abused her? Was this where he'd been conceived?

The Adam's apple on Leo's neck bobbed. He looked ashen, his handsome, aging face seeming mummified, leathery. "I'm still waiting for him to open that door and greet us." He raised his hand. "Wait. Any moment now..."

Silence fell around them. Everyone stared at the house. Worry tickled the back of Channing's neck. A raven cawed somewhere above, and wind whooshed through the black tree branches behind the cast-iron fence.

"That's his car." Leo nodded at the blood red bumper protruding from the snow. "No one dares to drive it but him."

But he was dead. Why did he need a reminder? Leo couldn't have gotten the time machine repaired, gone back in time, and stopped Dan's death...

Right?

Leo pushed past the gate and walked through the snow towards the house. He was bent over like a dark question mark, his arms shoved into the pockets of his wool coat.

As the rest of the group followed him, and Ella and Channing walked side by side, she leaned to him and whispered, "You have some serious explaining to do."

Not just explaining. Protecting. Something was wrong. Why had they come here? Why Dan's house?

"Just trust me," he whispered.

She scoffed. "That's goddamn difficult to do after today."

"I know." He searched her eyes. "Whatever happens, you are my priority."

For a bit, she didn't say anything. She looked straight ahead as she climbed up the stairs, digging her boots into the snow with each step. "We'll see."

He'd just opened his mouth to tell her she was, of course she was, but she hurried up in front of him and entered the mansion, and the shadows beyond the door swallowed her.

Channing cursed under his breath, speeding up after her. He slipped on something—a layer of ice under the snow—and he lost his balance for a moment, the world careening beneath him.

Someone caught him and steadied him. Leo, surprisingly strong, held him by the elbow. "Careful now. You don't want to fall and break your neck."

Channing nodded, although the unease spread through him like a disease. "Thanks."

Leo let go of him and entered the mansion. Channing followed.

Inside, a grand wooden staircase swept up to the floors above. The interior was surprisingly modern and sleek. As Leo flicked the switch and light flooded the entrance hall, the surfaces of the huge abstract paintings glimmered. The hardwood floor held no trace of dust. The place smelled like wood polish and cigarette smoke. Channing noticed a glass ashtray with several cigarette butts stood on the sideboard. Somewhere deeper inside the house, music switched on—smooth jazz.

His arm shot to the gun at the back of his pants, and Ella's hand jerked to the Glock Channing knew she had under her jacket.

"Is there someone in the house?" she asked in her cop voice.

Leo's eyes narrowed at her briefly. "That's how Dan liked it. There are sensors so that music starts when he comes in. I never changed it."

Some sort of household equipment beeped behind the walls.

"Come," Leo said and walked through an arched entryway to his right. He turned and threw over his shoulder, "You boys stay back."

They entered what looked like a chef's kitchen, gleaming stainless steel appliances, not a spot of grease or trace of dust. The fruit in the bowl on the island was fresh, and when Leo opened the fridge, it was fully stocked.

"How is this stuff here in the middle of a goddamn apocalypse?" Ella looked around. "Is someone living here?"

"No." Leo pressed on one of the buttons of the coffee machine and it whirred, grinding beans, and the scent of freshly ground coffee filled the kitchen. Leo retrieved a wooden plank from one of the cupboards and placed a selection of cheese on it.

He placed a piece in his mouth and chewed. "Gorgonzola was his favorite. Strange. I never liked it until he was gone. Now, it's the only cheese I like to eat."

He placed a bunch of grapes on the plank next to the cheese. Ella swallowed as she looked at it. With the food shortages and the trip into the Viking Age, she hadn't had fresh fruit for weeks. And she wasn't the only one. What about children who needed nutrients to grow? What about pregnant women? The elderly?

And yet, the Mafia had a stocked fridge in an empty house where no one lived.

Leo retrieved a large bread knife from the knife block and sliced a loaf of ciabatta on a cutting board. "His mother made the best homemade pasta. The best. All mothers are great at something, aren't they, Channing?"

The surface of the kitchen island was cool under Channing's hand as he took a seat at it. Had his mother's head ever landed on the edge of it, struck by Dan's hand? Had she ever tried to take that knife to protect herself?

Whether he wanted it or not, this house was part of his dark, perverse history. If his very existence was a mistake, this house was where it had probably happened.

Ella sat next to him and plucked a grape, put it into her mouth, and chewed. Her eyes closed briefly.

"Yes, all mothers are great at something," Channing said.

The knife knocked against the wooden board as Leo cut. "You can learn a lot about a man not just from the way his father is. But the way his mother is."

Channing's mother was a healer and the most selfless human being he knew. And yet, Channing was selfish, his ego driving every step. Was that his biological father's legacy? Odin and Thor, was he more similar to his violent father than he'd ever wanted to be?

The bread's crust crackled as Leo cut another piece. "I know who your mother was, Channing. But who is yours, Ella?"

Ella froze with another grape halfway to her mouth and looked at Channing. He saw Leo's reflection watching them in one of the cupboards.

Ella chewed slowly and swallowed. "I didn't know her well."

Leo lined up the slices of ciabatta carefully along the board. "Hmm. A woman with a lost mother."

Channing's fist clenched on his knee. "What does it matter?"

Leo cut through the middle of the line of bread slices. "Dan's mother was always there, always present. She breastfed him. He never went to a day care. Martha, poor thing, she had so many miscarriages, and he was her only one. Like a true

Italian mother, she wanted him to feel like a king. She'd never have abandoned him. Never."

He picked up the bread board, the knife still in his other hand, and brought it to the kitchen island.

"She also would have never betrayed the family." He held the board out to Ella and stared her straight in the eyes. "Not to the cops."

She picked up a piece of bread, bit, and chewed. Without faltering or lowering her gaze from his, she said, "I'd never betray anyone."

Her hand in her lap under the countertop clenched into a fist.

Leo laid the board on the island and placed the knife next to it, without removing his hand. "Do you know what we do to those that betray the vow?"

Ella swallowed. "You kill them?"

"No."

Channing knew the answer, and his blood froze. Fuck it all, a thousand ways and back. If only she hadn't followed him, Leo wouldn't be threatening Ted, Bryan, and Gloria. "She won't betray the family to the cops."

Leo tapped his thumb against the blade of the knife under his palm. "The biggest motivation to keep someone in line is often not threatening their own life. I'd give anything so that the killer would have taken my life instead of Dan's."

"Leo..." Channing growled.

Leo's cool gaze turned to him. "What would you do to keep hers?"

The answer was, he'd give anything.

Anything.

A realization hit him like a slap. Did that anything include giving up his relationship with her?

No. That was exactly what he'd fought for this whole time,

wasn't it? If he didn't have her, he didn't have home. This whole time, his whole life, he hadn't belonged anywhere. He wasn't a Viking in the Viking Age. He wasn't a proper modern man in the twenty-first century.

The only person he felt like himself with was her. The only person who was like him...was Ella.

She was the very essence of his blood, the matter of his soul, the nucleus of his cells.

"Stop threatening my future wife."

"Calm down, you silly pup. You're just like your dead father, all angry outbursts and short temper."

His stomach churned, bile rising. *Like his father?* He was nothing like his father. And he wanted Ella of all people to know that. He looked at her, but she was keeping her eyes on Leo.

Leo turned to the wine fridge and took out a black bottle. "Don't start throwing bottles against the walls like he did."

Leo opened another cabinet and took out three elegant wineglasses and placed them on the kitchen island in front of Ella and Channing. "This whole business...the Mafia...it's all nothing without my son." He stabbed the cover of the wine bottle with a small knife and cut it. "I built it all for the family. For him. For his kids." He looked at Channing. "For you."

Channing's jaw tightened. *For you...* He didn't need it, any of it. It was all built on the misery of others.

Leo bored the bottle opener into the cork, every turn making a squeak. "Do you ever think about destiny?"

Channing stopped breathing, and he knew Ella did, too. She was frozen, so still she could be a statue made of flesh and blood.

"All the time," she said.

Leo pulled the cork, and it released with a pop.

"Do you ever wonder how your life would have been

different had you been in a certain place at a certain time? What would you have done to change your circumstances?"

Ella inhaled sharply. "More than you know."

Leo poured the red wine into the three glasses. "This was his favorite wine. Tenuta dell'Ornellaia. Almost a thousand dollars a bottle. He'd often drink it with coke suppliers to sweeten the deal. The Colombians love chianti."

He pushed two glasses towards Ella and Channing, then picked up his own and rotated it, watching the dark liquid roll around the glass, flowing down the walls in purple teardrops.

"I miss the simpler times when it was all about the coke. This weapons trade is a more complicated business."

He brought the glass to his nose and inhaled, closing his eyes.

"*Dio*, this smells like my son," he murmured, then looked at Channing. "The Colombians, they don't fear me like they feared him. No wine can sweeten the deal now. Luca would have never wanted to go rogue with Dan here. My son was the iron fist that held it all together. That held me together."

He took a small sip, sucking in air through a round O, then swallowed, closing his eyes.

"Dan, Dan..." He dropped his head and whispered, "I swear, he's still somewhere in this house, watching us." He glanced around, then looked at Channing. "He doesn't even feel dead. He'll never be dead."

Channing's fingers clenched around the glass. "But he is."

Leo shook his head. "That's what I mean by destiny. You had to be born in another time to come back here and create the time machine. With the time machine, I'll go back and stop his death. I'll kill the bastard that murdered him."

It had been Channing's mother. Leo would kill Mia, who'd been pregnant with Channing at the time.

Leo looked at Ella. "That's the kind of family you're

marrying into, sweetheart. A family that hates the cops, makes their own law and their own destiny. A family that defies death." He raised his glass. "Can you stomach it?"

Ella raised her own glass, looking straight into Leo's eyes. "You bet I can."

As the three of them clinked glasses and sipped the wine, Channing thought she definitely could.

But how long would it last until Leo found out that Channing had no intention to let him use the time machine—that his goal was to destroy it?

And how long would it take Leo to find out Ella was a cop and her father was an ex-cop? How long until Leo would kill them?

He'd rather cut his chest open and tear his own heart out than let that happen.

The only way to protect Ella from his grandfather was to do just that.

Because that's what breaking up with her would be like.

EIGHTEEN

The way back was dead silence.

He was a Mafia man.

She was a cop.

He may or may not have killed Nick Murphy, the guy she'd grown up with, the guy she had dated.

He'd betrayed her. He'd lied to her. And now, not only was she in mortal danger, but her family was as well.

And the police couldn't do shit about it. Because, as Dad had said so well, they were weaker than kittens.

Ella glared from behind the windows at the snowed-in streets passing by. Under normal circumstances, the drive from Back Bay to downtown took about ten minutes. Now, slowed down by the snow, every minute ticked past like an eternity.

Broken-in buildings with boarded-up windows flashed by. In the alleys between buildings, people huddled around fires burning in trash cans. A body lay in the snow. Two men were talking, then waved their arms, arguing, fingers stabbing at each other.

If Ella didn't do something to stop Surtr and the Mafia,

arguments like that would soon lead to shootings. They were feeding world conflicts, wars, truly contributing to the end of the world.

And Channing was contributing to the chaos, this time by choice.

Pain tore her soul apart. She'd had this wound her whole life because she'd believed her mother had betrayed her, abandoned her.

Channing had made her whole. He'd shown her she didn't have to feel that way. He'd made her believe she could be happy. She could be loved.

Her wound had started healing. It had scabbed over and grown a tender new skin. And now it had been slashed open again.

She was still terrified of trusting people.

But she'd trusted him.

And he'd made her bleed.

As they drove through downtown and passed the police station, she saw even more people huddling next to the building. They were hoping for protection, but it would never come.

Bodies blackened the snow here and there. People didn't survive frostbite, hunger, and hypothermia.

She looked at Channing, who watched out of the window with an expression as hard as rock. Was he feeling guilty? Did he think this was all because of him?

And a treacherous voice whispered, *Do you? What if nothing would stop Ragnarök—nothing, except for his death?*

Part of her ached to cuddle up into his big, strong arms, hug him, whisper it all was going to be all right.

Only, she didn't know it would be.

They were left in the garage of his building. When the car disappeared through the gate, Channing marched to his car.

Without turning, he took out the key. "Come on, Ella. I'll take you home."

"I need to pick up my car."

"I'll bring it to you. I don't want you anywhere near the Mafia."

She didn't move. She'd held on to her self-control for hours, told herself to keep it together or the Mafia would kill them. She couldn't afford to fall apart.

But now that they were safe, a sinking feeling of devastation flooded her. It all came crashing back into her psyche. The shooting. The bodies. Nick's dead body. And Channing, with a gun and a sword walking by Leo Esposito's side. The scent of the garage—gas and oil and rubber—made her feel sick.

"Did you kill him?" she rasped. "Nick? You told me you'd kill him back by the New Family Max."

His eyes were dark, haunted. "Would it change anything if I did?"

"I don't know." Hurt was pressing on her lungs, making it hard to breathe. "You're a made man now, aren't you?"

He nodded.

"That was what you didn't want to tell me?"

Another nod.

"What are you doing to us, Channing? Against my better judgment, against my duty as a police officer, against what my gut and my logical mind told me, I fell in love with you. I trusted you. I wanted a future with you."

His eyes were fogged with pain. "Wanted...?"

She gave a sharp exhale, her breath a cloud of condensation. "I'm still a detective. You were a CEO who did one bad thing and imported a nuclear reactor to save your family. I could have lived with that, reckless though it was."

He took a step towards her. "Ella—"

"Now, you're a proper criminal. A gun trafficker. Maybe

even a murderer. Whether you wanted it or not, you are the force of Ragnarök now, Channing."

He dug his fingers into his hair. He looked like a wounded animal that didn't know how to keep fighting. "You're leaving me."

Not a question. A statement.

"What am I supposed to do? I'll have to report what I've witnessed. I'll have to report you as a member of the Mafia. You'll be charged with more serious stuff than importing nuclear material. How could you have not thought about that?"

He looked like he was being sentenced to death. He nodded. "You're doing what I didn't have the guts to do, Ella. You and your family are safer away from me."

You are everything. Everything... His words rang in her head.

He pressed the button and five cars down, his SUV blinked.

He opened the passenger door and turned to her. His eyes were dark, expression unchanging, like the statue of a war god. He looked at her as though she wasn't the woman he'd swore his loyalty to. Not the woman he'd said he wanted to marry.

Not the woman he'd said he'd save the world for.

But like she was no one.

"You promised me. You swore an oath to me. You said your loyalty would always be to me."

Hurt flickered in his eyes, then it was gone. He straightened his shoulders. "And it is."

"No, it's not."

"It's just a matter of time before he finds out you really are a cop. He might be digging into your history as we speak."

She hit him in the middle of his chest with the side of her fist. "We were in this together. I thought you wanted a future with me."

He kept drilling her with his dark eyes.

"It seems I was wrong. I won't be your future. I'll be your end. As long as you're with me, you'll always be in danger. And your family."

She could take the fucking danger. She could protect herself and her family.

She couldn't take betrayal.

"Every word you spoke was a lie. Your oath. Your promises. Your...your *I love you*."

He stood immobile, his mouth a straight, white line in his short beard. His nostrils kept flaring in a quick rhythm as he sucked in air.

She stepped back. That one step between them was like an abyss. "I'm glad it's over, really."

He blinked. Once. Twice.

"You just saved me years. Even if we'd defeated Ragnarök, eventually, I'd have realized I couldn't trust you. That I made a mistake with you. You'll be in prison, Channing."

Before the paper-thin barrier of her self-control was torn through, she turned and walked towards the exit. She didn't feel the concrete floor under her shoes. She didn't see a column and bumped into it with her bad shoulder, pain exploding through her body.

She heard his steps behind her. "Ella, let me drive you back home."

"I'll find my own way back. And don't bother about my car. I'll get it myself."

She'd be damned if she let him see her pain.

As she stepped into the frozen air, she thought that now that she'd lost the man she loved, she didn't care if the world ended.

The only thing that would keep her from letting that happen was her family.

She still had to stop this for Ted, for her dad, for Gloria, for Uncle Mo and little Pamela and for everyone else in her family and in the world.

She would concentrate on doing a good job for the police, trying to keep the world safe, and working on accessing and controlling her powers.

She called Ricardo. "Can you pick me up?"

NINETEEN

Channing grabbed the wheel and stared at the white wall of the garage before him. Since Ella left, he'd gotten back into his car and had been sitting there, trying to force himself to drive.

Every movement hurt. Breathing hurt. The endless sucking wound in his chest radiated pain like a fifth-degree burn.

He saw the incredible pain he'd caused her, and it killed him like poison injected right into the core of his soul.

He'd hated that he had to hurt her, but he knew he could end this. He knew he could end Ragnarök.

And once he'd done that and the danger was gone, he'd help the police to end the Mafia.

Then, with her and her family safe, he'd drop on his knees before her and beg her to take him back. Eventually she'd learn to trust him again.

But she may never forgive him.

Still. That wouldn't be as bad as having her death on his hands.

So he'd have to live with this for the rest of his life.

But now, he had to act. Now that he'd gained the trust of

his grandfather, he could finally get into action and destroy the fucking time machine. He pressed the ignition button on his SUV, ignoring the heavy, unyielding pain at the bottom of his stomach.

He drove into the port.

As he drove, he turned on the radio. "Surtr Enterprises, the top manufacturer of materials used for weapons and explosives, was discovered to have fulfilled large orders for criminal organizations all over the world. Government officials speculate these organizations are growing due to what scientists have unofficially called the 'climate apocalypse,' an extreme global cooling event that started several weeks ago..."

Channing blinked. Ella was right. By joining the Mafia, he had truly become a force for Ragnarök. He'd supported Surtr Enterprises and the gun trade. In the stories of Ragnarök he'd heard as a child, Surtr was a fire giant. He would set the whole world on fire.

That was exactly what Surtr Enterprises was doing.

And so was he.

But not for long. If he destroyed the time machine, it would all stop.

He hoped.

The Mafia goon guarding the gate let him in without a problem. Like Leo had promised, everyone knew who Channing was.

The Mafia prince.

Getting inside building M05 was more difficult. Questions were raised, and he told the goons guarding the building he had been asked to consult with the scientists about how to make the spindle work.

When he descended the stairs to the basement, a thinner version of Georgina with bloodshot eyes looked up at him from her laptop. Munchie was playing tic-tac-toe on the whiteboard. He wasn't munching on anything.

When Channing reached the bottom, he looked up. Three dark figures watched him from above, machine guns still in their arms, then they were gone.

"Boss..." said Munchie.

He didn't look great, either. Dark shadows stained the skin under his eyes, and his shoulders slouched over his thin frame.

Georgina rose. "What are you doing here?"

Channing looked over the spindle. It was giant and imposing, and it was the reason for all this. The memory of Ella touching the spindle and disappearing flashed through his mind.

"I came because we need to destroy this," he said. "You must know how."

Georgina and Munchie looked at each other.

"What about Leonardo? Doesn't he want it to work?"

Channing glanced up at the entry into the lab. He didn't see anyone. But that didn't mean they weren't listening just out of sight.

He turned to the scientists and said in a low voice, "We cannot let him use the time machine. And to stop all this...Ragnarök...I think that the time machine lies at the very core of it all."

They looked at each other. He took in a deep breath and told them everything. How he was conceived in the twenty-first century and born in the ninth. How he grew up with the Vikings. The prophecy and the rest.

It felt good to open up to the two people who'd been paramount in making the time machine. And when he finished, Georgina tapped her finger against her lower lip, frowning at him like he was a puzzle she was trying to solve. Munchie was silent, staring blankly at the whiteboard.

"So..." he said, pointing at it with his marker. "That would actually explain the odd writing on our whiteboard. The part of the formula that appeared one night."

"What would explain it?" Georgina turned to him.

"It must be one of those...Norns or whatever that wrote it."

"That makes no sense," Georgina said. "If they weave the destiny of men and gods, they wouldn't change it, would they?"

"I don't know. I didn't think they did. But they also sent my mother through time."

"It could be your girlfriend, Mr. Hakonson," said Georgina. Channing had told them about Ella's strange powers, too. That her mother was a Norn. "I bet she can do more than we all realize."

Girlfriend... The word was like acid poured over him. She wasn't his girlfriend anymore. Longing for her burned him.

"Right. Well. Whoever did or didn't write it, if we destroy it..." Munchie said. "Shit, boss. But does that mean you can never return to your family? The whole point of making this..." He gestured at the spindle.

Another wave of pain made Channing's heart ache. "I know. It has to be done."

Georgina gave him an empathetic smile.

Munchie stood up and walked to the spindle. "We definitely can't let Leo Esposito go back in time and stop Daniel from dying. Then it's entirely possible you wouldn't exist...or you would be a two-year-old."

Channing shook his head. "That is not an option. We have to figure out how to destroy the time machine. How far are you from fixing it?"

Georgina and Munchie exchanged a look, and Munchie took a few steps towards him and said in a low voice, "It's not broken."

Georgina smiled and shrugged. "He doesn't know how to operate it, anyway."

Hope blossomed in Channing's chest. "But why did you decide to lie?"

Munchie shook his head. "I'm not helping the fucking Mafia, boss. No way. No matter what they're up to, it's wrong."

"But what about your families? He threatened them."

"As long as we keep pretending like we're working, we're fine," Georgina said.

Channing cleared his throat. "You two brave, stupid heroes. But you're right, you did well by not letting him use the machine. Yes. Okay. So what, do I get an ax and just hammer at the thing?"

Munchie chuckled. "I'd like to see you try. Gold is a soft metal, but I highly doubt you can really damage it enough with an ax."

Georgina added, "It has to be irreversible, something that can't be easily repaired. Something without which Leo wouldn't even be able to reproduce the machine."

"Does it have some sort of core or something?" Channing asked.

"No core."

Channing looked it over. The runes... Georgina, Munchie, and he had learned pretty much everything they could about Norse mythology. He'd remembered some of the runes from the rune stone next to Lomdalen and others from the spindle in the hands of the Norn...Ella's mom. Now they decorated the time machine's huge golden spindle and apparently gave it power.

"So what then?" he said. "Melt it? How would that even work?"

Munchie leaned forward over the back of the chair in front of him. "I have an idea."

Georgina smiled at him. "Is it what I'm thinking?"

"What are you thinking?" asked Channing.

Munchie chuckled, his eyes sparkling. "This might sound crazy. And there are a lot of factors that might interfere with the process."

Channing crossed his arms over his chest. "Okay. What is it?"

"This is where years of research about gold, and Norse runes, and the Norns themselves come into play."

"Sure."

"Have you ever asked yourself, why gold?"

Channing shrugged. "I guess it's a metal that doesn't corrode or rust. It's pretty long-lasting, isn't it?"

Munchie straightened and paced the length of the room. "Exactly. Exactly right. It doesn't get damaged easily. It's impossible to destroy it completely without radiation. It's possible to damage it physically with force, but it'll only leave indents and deform it. It's possible to melt it, of course, but it's pretty damn hard to dissolve it. And yet, there's one liquid that can."

"What, dissolve gold?"

Georgina grinned. "Yes. Aqua regia."

"Aqua regia?"

"It's Latin for *royal water*," Georgina said. "It's a mix of nitric acid and hydrochloric acid. It does dissolve gold but very, very slowly. The time machine is two tons."

Munchie nodded. "And aqua regia won't destroy the gold. Just dissolve it."

Channing looked between them. "But by dissolving the spindle, the time machine will be gone."

"Yes," Munchie said.

"Okay. Can we do it?" asked Channing.

Georgina drummed her fingers against the table once. "Even if you dissolve it, it can be re-created."

"Do you have any documentation left?"

Georgina pointed at her laptop. "Yes, of course."

Channing nodded. "Destroy it. Burn any trace of it."

Georgina looked at Munchie, who nodded. "Okay."

Munchie cleared his throat. "You know, there's only one way to completely get rid of it."

Channing sighed. "We won't use the nuclear reactor to destroy it. It's too dangerous."

Munchie nodded. "Exactly."

"Okay. So how much aqua regia do we need and how exactly do we do it?"

Georgina started typing on her laptop. After a few moments, she looked up at him. "You won't like my answer. You'll need to flood the basement with it. Then the only way to melt the gold quickly is to heat the aqua regia up. Or wait for days for it to dissolve. I'm guessing you don't have days before Leo realizes what's going on."

"You're guessing right."

"Then the *only* way to generate enough heat is to use the nuclear reactor."

The giant golden spindle lay on its side on the basement floor, the ceiling lights gleaming off its shiny surface. They had taken it off the axis to be able to cover more of its surface with less liquid. Five days had passed in preparations, searching for a supplier with enough aqua regia, then waiting for them to collect enough fuel to send the trucks.

All the while, more snow covered the world, the sun dulled like an antique gold plate, and more wolves came into the city. The piles of frozen bodies next to the police station rose.

The goons had let Georgina, Munchie, and Channing enter the basement lab without a problem. He'd told them he was helping get the spindle fixed.

And still, uneasiness crawled up Channing's spine. If he was honest with himself, there was part of him that wanted that trust. That wanted that friendship and that belonging to a family, to a clan. That wanted the sense of community he'd known in the Viking Age and craved all fourteen years in the twenty-first century.

But it was only a tiny part of him, he told himself. He knew what he had to do. Watching the world die and crumble around him wasn't an option.

Georgina had said to Leo Esposito that they needed to get the gold cleaned using acid so that they could repair the damages and smooth out the runes. Then, she promised, they could use it and get his son back. But the acid, Georgina explained, was deadly to breathe, and they needed to keep everyone out of the building. Upstairs, a truck with a tank full of aqua regia beeped frantically as it backed up towards the open entrance of the basement pit. Channing looked around for one last time, searching for anything important he might have forgotten here.

"All of the papers and our laptops and equipment have been taken out," Georgina said.

"Looks like we got everything," Munchie said, looking around.

Channing's gaze landed on the giant concrete cylinder that contained the nuclear reactor. "Not everything."

His back covered in cold sweat as he imagined what would happen if the three tanks of aqua regia went through concrete and entered the nuclear reactor. That would destroy the gold completely, along with the whole city of Boston.

"Are you sure the concrete won't be affected right away?" Channing asked.

"Serious damage can only happen after months of exposure," Georgina reassured him. "With the right amount of heat, the gold will be dissolved by tomorrow morning, and after that, we pump it back into the trucks and off they go."

Channing sighed and mumbled. "And when Leo finds out we deceived him...Odin's ass. Promise me you'll be on your way out with the trucks the moment it's all done."

"Don't worry, boss," Munchie said. "He'll never know you had anything to do with this idea. If this can indeed stop the hell that's going on in the world, it's all going to be worth it."

"But what about your families?" asked Channing.

"They'll be with us," Georgina said. "We have a plan."

Something metallic bumped against the wall and the three of them looked up. A big tube hung suspended from the tank.

"Are you good for me to start?" the driver called.

"We're coming up," Channing said.

When the three of them stood dressed in hazmat suits next to the truck, the driver, who also put on one of the protective garments, switched on the pump, and golden-orange liquid poured from the tube and into the basement. Even through the hazmat helm, Channing could smell a scent resembling chlorine. The acidic water splashed against the concrete walls and floor. No hissing came, no fumes, just the deadly splashing and the roar of the engine of the truck.

Channing knew this was the end of any chance to use the time machine and go back in time again to be with his family. The faces of his mother, his father, and his brother and sister, whom he'd last seen in the ninth century, would forever be imprinted on his mind and his heart.

A fair price to pay to keep Ella alive.

And a minuscule price to pay to save the world.

Still, a dark sense of loss enveloped him.

The liquid poured, slowly covering the spindle inch by inch. The entrance door banged, and someone peered from outside, but Georgina waved her hands frantically, indicating the person should leave right away.

But the door opened, and Leo marched forward, angrily covering the space.

"I'll deal with him," Channing said and hurried towards his grandfather.

When he reached Leo, he took him by the elbow, turned

him around, and led him back to the entrance. "You can't be in here."

"What's going on?" he demanded as he walked. "Why is there a truck pouring the stuff in there?" He looked back over his shoulder. "I thought this was supposed to be a quick cleaning. We have an order from Surtr Enterprises coming in today. It was supposed to be stored here until it can be loaded onto a container ship."

"It is a quick cleaning," Channing said as he opened the door for Leo and pretty much pushed him out of the building. "But this stuff is toxic. It can't be handled directly. What's the shipment?"

"Ammonium nitrate," said Leo. "They use it in bombs. We can load a whole container ship with that shit. Need as many warehouses as we can get. It's in demand everywhere—Colombia, South Africa, Russia."

Channing's stomach dropped. "Why do they need so much?"

Leo crossed his arms over his chest. "What planet do you live on, Channing? It's the fucking end of the world. If you can't protect yourself, you're done. In the coming days and months, weapons and explosives will be as valuable as food to stay alive. I'd be a bad businessman if I missed an opportunity like that."

Channing pictured the whole world burning. Flames reaching into the sky.

"You can't store that stuff here with those other acids in the same building. No one can even be inside without a suit on."

Suspicion flashed through Leo's eyes. "But why so much?"

"I don't know. I'm not a scientist. But if those guys say this is how much is needed, it's how much they need. They know what they're doing."

"Are you sure? Something's not right."

"If you want to put on a suit and watch them clean, you're welcome to do so."

Leo looked him up and down. "Why are you here, anyway?" his grandfather asked.

"It's still my port. I need to know what's going on."

Leo took a deep breath. "I know better than to interfere where I have no idea what's going on."

"Look. It'll take a few days and then the thing will be good to go, and you can go back in time."

And save your son...my father... The words didn't manage to get past the rock lodged in Channing's throat.

"Okay." He clapped Channing on the shoulder. "Keep an eye on them. There's something bugging me about those two."

Hours later, the gold was bubbling and dissolving in the orange acid like sugar candy in water. It was quiet in building M05. The truck engine was off. Nothing whirred. No footsteps echoed from the concrete walls.

The only sound was the golden bubbles in the aqua regia whispering as they melted the doom of the world away like the sun melted snow.

By the morning, Channing knew nothing would be left of the two tons of gold. Then they'd pump the liquid back into the truck and get the hell out. He had only to sneak Munchie and Georgina away in time. Then they'd be able to get into an MIT lab and neutralize the acid bit by bit, after which the liquid would be safe and the gold would be recovered. Two tons of gold had cost him over a hundred million dollars. The plan now was to use that money to get food and medicine to those in need, to help in whatever way he could.

If he was the reason for Ragnarök, this was one small way to make amends.

Of course, he wouldn't be able to bring back the thousands of people who had lost their lives.

Deep sadness corroded his heart.

A shadow appeared from behind him, and he looked around. One of the goons was looking into the basement pit, his eyes wide. "Where's the giant golden spindle?" he said.

Channing's heart dropped into his stomach. "You're not supposed to be here!"

"Is that everything that's left?" the man asked, staring at the bubbling, golden stump. "Leo was right to ask me to come and look."

The man put his wrist to his mouth and started to say something, no doubt to alert the rest of the guards. Channing had to do something. He hit the man in the stomach with his fist and the man grunted and doubled up in pain.

The hazmat suit slowed Channing down, restraining his movements, but he swung again as hard as he could. The punch caught the goon in the side of his face. The man grunted and swung his fist at Channing in return but lost his balance and plummeted down into the pool of acid. He yelled in agony as his skin reddened and bubbled. He splashed with his arms, trying to grab on to something. Channing ran to the metal stairs leading down, but the bottom steps disappeared into the acid. He tugged at the metal tube that still hung from the truck into the basement and thrust it towards the man.

He saw it and made the wide movements with his arms to swim towards the pipe, but he swallowed the acid and stopped screaming and gave out a terrible gurgling sound. In a few moments, he grew silent and floated in the quietly bubbling gold and acid.

Channing sank down to the floor, his stomach sick as the royal water decomposed human flesh into nothing. Cold sweat dripped down his back. Another life taken.

How many more would need to die before he'd abandon his selfish determination to be happy?

When Georgina and Munchie returned, Channing didn't say anything. There was a chunk of gold left the size of an office chair. Would that count as remnants of the time machine, or could he leave the piece? The man would soon be missed.

No, he decided. They'd come this far.

"How long still, do you think?" he asked.

"An hour," Georgina said.

"Good."

When the last bit of it was dissolved, they called back the driver, who started the engine, and the liquid began to get pumped back into the tank. Munchie and Georgina had made sure it was big enough to accommodate the additional volume. As Georgina had suggested, it took another hour or so.

Channing thought they might just get away without any further issues. But as the last bits of the orange-gold liquid were sucked up, the door to the building opened and Leonardo marched in with five goons behind him.

"Get into the truck, quick," Channing said firmly and, removing his hazmat suit, ran after them. The acrid scent of chlorine hit him in the face.

"Channing!" called Leo. "Where are you going? Stop!"

Running footsteps sounded after him as he climbed into the cabin of the truck. The engine revved and the driver hit the gas, swinging around and heading for the exit. Channing looked back from the window.

Wild-eyed, Leo stared at the empty pit of the basement, which, no doubt, glistened with the remnants of the royal water mixed with liquid gold. He roared. An animal cry of a wounded predator that had just lost its pup.

"You will die!" he roared out, raising his gun. An onslaught of shots followed the truck, hitting the tank.

"Faster!" Channing yelled to the driver as bullets kept hitting the metal.

As they drove out of building Mo5, the sunrise over the city was pink and golden, a warm blush of spring, not the coldness of winter.

Only as the truck passed through the gate and left the port did Channing breathe a sigh of relief.

The time machine was gone, just like they had planned.

Maybe Ragnarök would be gone with it, too.

And, no matter how much he hated it, part of him did ache with the regret of betraying his only grandfather.

But he shoved it away. With the spindle gone, the world could recover. And Ella and her family had a future.

It was good she wasn't with him anymore. He had a dangerous, furious enemy at his heels.

TWENTY-ONE

Ella's heart—or whatever was left of it—was jumping out of her chest as she, Ricardo, and a squad of five other cops rode the elevator up to Channing's penthouse.

Ten days ago, he had disappeared from her world. Ten days ago, she had found out he wasn't who she'd thought he was. Ten days ago, he'd shattered her heart and broken her trust.

She'd broken his trust in return when she'd filed the police report about the shooting in Quincy she'd witnessed. When she'd gotten a warrant for his arrest. As far as the police and the FBI were concerned, Channing Hakonson was with the Mafia.

Gun running and murder had been added to his charges.

It had killed her to do this. How many times had she saved his life, and he saved hers?

But when they arrived at the penthouse, the door was open...

Every single piece of furniture had been turned over. The beautiful modern Nordic wall art lay broken on the floor. The long fireplace in the center of the room Ella had always thought about as the central hearth had bullet holes in it. Polished marble chips and pieces lay around it. The glass in the kitchen appliances was broken and shattered. The drawers in the side-boards were open and their contents spilled out on the floor. Did he fight someone? Did someone want to send him a message?

As she stepped inside the apartment, her gun drawn, the cracking glass under her feet sounded like bombs exploding in the silence.

She'd find him dead, she felt certain. She'd find him dead somewhere inside the apartment.

She couldn't breathe. Couldn't move. Couldn't think.

Images of Channing under King Harald's ax... Him wounded on the snow... Him being beaten by the crowd in the port... Her dreams—every night, every single time she drifted into a short sleep—the world was ending, the Vikings were there, dead, and she held the sword at his neck.

Death came at him, chased him constantly.

And now, it had arrived.

She shook as she stepped forward.

No, no, no. She didn't want him to die. She was angry and hurt. He'd betrayed her.

But she still loved him. Despite the hurt, seeing him dead would kill her, too.

They moved through the trashed apartment. There, on the couch that had been turned over, she had sat by his side and sutured his wound. There, up the stairs, in his bedroom, she'd seen his glorious body for the first time.

But he wasn't there. He wasn't in his bedroom, nor in his archive room, where the originals of the Icelandic sagas lay torn and broken among the shards of archival glass boxes. Nor was he in his study.

They searched through his things, took his computer, but didn't find any clues or proof of his participation in Mafia business. No guns, only swords and scramasaxes, which were Viking short swords.

The fact that they didn't find him gave her some relief. But it didn't mean he wasn't dead.

With every day that passed, things in the city and the world continued to improve.

The leaden, icy clouds parted and let the sun through. The air warmed up. The snow melted. Green grass appeared on the lawns, and trees stood naked and vulnerable.

As the snow melted, roads cleared. Slowly, in the warm parts of the globe, greenhouses started working again. Food deliveries increased, and grocery stores now had more fresh bread, somewhat beaten-up and wilted vegetables, and dairy, which had for the most part gone over the expiration date but was fine nevertheless.

People could breathe again.

Only Ella couldn't celebrate like everyone else. Every time she sucked in air, pain tore her chest apart. As though her very heart had been cut in half and bled like an open wound.

If Ragnarök had ended, he was dead. And if he was dead... she was finished. She'd never recover.

They must have killed him—the Mafia or the Vikings, probably. That was why the sun was shining, the snow was melting, the wolves were gone, and food was being delivered again. That was why they got fewer 911 calls, why people were in a better mood, why the sense of relief and hope was everywhere, like the scent of spring.

That must be why she'd had those dreams of Ragnarök. Of him, dying by her hand.

You are everything, he'd told her. *Everything.*

What if he'd done all of that so that he could sacrifice himself? So that the Mafia would kill him?

No. They had agreed to fight, to find a way to stop this and be together.

Only she'd broken up with him.

So there was no reason for him to fight, to stop Ragnarök.

Oh, God, what if he'd gotten himself killed because she broke up with him?

What if he'd died because of her?

What if the world was finally safe, only without Channing it would forever be empty?

She stopped trying to manipulate time because it reminded her of how she'd failed. Every time she allowed herself to think even for a second, pain tore at her.

She supposed this was Ragnarök. The end of the world. The end of love. The end of hope.

The end of them.

She went through every morgue in the city, looked through every ditch, looked around the Surtr warehouse, even considered meeting with Leo Esposito...

Only then, she'd be putting her family in more danger, and she couldn't do that to them.

But she kept looking. She was surveilling the port. Another team was surveilling Surtr Enterprises' headquarters in another location in Quincy, a pristine, modern office building, unlike the abandoned warehouse they'd used to traffic weapons undetected. Now that there were fewer crimes and emergency calls, the police were able to spare some officers. Though it would take a long time to get the city back to normal.

She was barely sleeping at all now. The moment she drifted off, that dream came, with the fires at the port, and the Vikings and the police dead, and her holding the sword at Channing's neck.

And she'd wake up.

Sometimes she felt like her body did things on its own.

Poured coffee and drank it without tasting anything. Moved her feet. Talked.

Only, she wasn't there. That thing...the soul...or whatever it was that made her *her* wasn't inside her anymore.

And she had this constant pressure, a pain, a tension in her chest. As though someone was sitting on her rib cage and she had to push against that weight to breathe.

Her only distraction was police work and driving Dad to the hospital for cancer treatments.

There was a tiny spark of hope somewhere in her soul that if they hadn't found the body yet, maybe he wasn't dead. That maybe he had stopped Ragnarök but was still alive.

And she had to find him. She had to find him in any case.

It was three weeks after their breakup that she had her first day off duty, and she went downtown. In three days was Ted's thirteenth birthday, and she wanted to buy him a present. The poor boy kept asking where Channing was every day, and she replied he'd had to leave for a while. Every time she did, her heart burst all over again, as though a grenade had exploded in her chest.

And each time, she saw the joy fade in his eyes a little. He really liked Channing.

So did she.

So it was time to cheer him up. Gloria planned to do a Rolf-themed cake, and Ella was headed to a bookstore she knew had the comic books he loved.

Walking down busy Washington Street, heels against the sidewalk, she enjoyed the warm sunrays on her face. A small mercy. Anything to distract her from the pain in her heart.

After the unprecedented cold, it still felt a bit strange to be wearing only a light autumn coat and a scarf. The feel of spring was in the air, even though it was now winter. Around her, people walked and talked. Some shops were open. Others that had been damaged were being repaired. Only three blocks away was Channing's skyscraper, and she'd go there to see if she might catch a glimpse of him nearby after she got the comic book for Ted.

She entered the shop and found one of the issues she knew he didn't have yet. She paid, but as she said goodbye and turned, she hit a wall.

A warm, hard wall that smelled like leather and manly musk and clean skin and that cologne that was both modern and masculine.

She staggered back and strong hands gripped her just above her elbows and steadied her.

Channing stared at her with such intensity, with so much pain and longing, that she felt like she might combust.

Her stomach flipped and sank to her feet. Was she having one of her dreams? She studied him closely, not quite sure if she should believe he was real.

He didn't look like himself. For one thing, he wasn't in a suit. He was in a Harvard hoodie. His long hair was hidden under a baseball cap. His beard was long; he probably hadn't trimmed it since she'd last seen him.

"Channing," she whispered, barely audible. "Are you really here...alive...?"

He nodded and glanced at the cashier, a young woman who was staring at them with curiosity, and looked away.

"Can we talk, please?"

She should arrest him. She should call Ricardo, call for backup. She didn't have her gun, but she could call 911 and get Ricardo here.

"Where have you been?" she asked, her throat clenching.

Her arms tingled. God, she wanted to hug him, bury her face in his neck, kiss him, inhale him, cling to him, have him wrap his arms around her.

"Long story. Can we just please sit somewhere and talk? Please?"

His chest was rising and falling quickly. His eyes were dark, and they were on her, devouring her like no one and nothing else existed. Heat spread through her. How could this man whom she still loved, who made her knees weak, who brightened the world around her be a criminal? A cold-blooded killer?

Who lied to her, abandoned her, and broke her trust.

She leaned closer to him and lowered her voice. "You know the police have a warrant for your arrest? You know the FBI is looking for you?"

"I suspected as much. They're not the worst people looking for me."

She frowned. "Who else is looking for you?"

"Not here. Is your uncle's pub still empty?"

She nodded.

"Let's go."

Uncle Maurice's pub, Mo's, was a five-minute walk down the street. Channing walked near her but not next to her. She turned in to the alley where she and Channing had once looked for refuge during a snowstorm and he had fought Vikings who had come through time to kill him.

She found the hidden key and unlocked the pub. Inside it was dark and dusty, just like she remembered. The door behind them closed, and they were in semidarkness. Sunlight fought through two small dirt-covered windows, barely illuminating the pub.

It looked just like when they'd been here during the snowstorm. The dark wood furniture, the scent of beer and wine. Even the glasses she and Channing had used still stood on the bar.

There was enough light to see his face. He was tense and

looked like he was in physical pain. She leaned against the entrance door, torn between her desire to cling to him and her duty to arrest him.

"It's over," he said. "Ragnarök. It's over."

"I thought it was. I thought you were dead. That your death was the reason it was over."

"I didn't need to die. I just needed to destroy the time machine."

Her face went limp. "You did?"

Yet another betrayal. She was supposed to use the spindle to go back in time and change things. That was the plan. With the golden spindle, she could have made it so that none of this destruction, none of these deaths would have happened. She was sure of it. But he had removed that option without even speaking to her about it.

"That's why I joined the Mafia. That's why I took the oath. That's why I lied to you. All of that was for you...for us."

She snorted. "You killed Nick and all those other men for me, too?"

"I didn't kill Nick, Ella. I didn't kill anyone in that warehouse. I've killed before, in the Viking Age. I killed Ragnar, and I killed Náli. You saw that. But I didn't kill Nick."

Something released in her, a tension in her solar plexus unlocked, and it was as though she could finally breathe again.

She gave out a half sigh, half sob, and she pressed a palm to her mouth.

"You didn't kill anyone?"

He shook his head and took a step closer. "No." His voice was soft, almost soothing. "I had to prove myself to my grandfather by dealing with one of the gun distributors who owed the family money. When I saw Nick, I realized he was from the mob. I knew it was a takeover, a dirty bloodbath. The Irish mob wanted to destroy the Mafia and take over the business with Surtr. They came to kill us all, especially Leo."

She let out another sob. She didn't know if she fully believed him.

But she knew in her heart he was telling the truth.

"After that, Leo trusted me fully. I talked to Munchie and Georgina about how to destroy the time machine to stop Leo from bringing Daniel back. We filled the lab with aqua regia, which dissolved the gold. We pumped it back into the truck and ran. Thankfully, Munchie and Georgina managed to escape right after we delivered the truck to MIT. They should be deep in the Midwest. Georgina has relatives there."

Ella was shaking. She was trying to stop her tremors by locking her knees and her elbows, but they were still shaking. He came to her and gently cupped her face with his hands. His eyes were dark and warm, and his lips were right there, and his scent was in her nostrils.

"Leo wants to kill me. I broke my oath to him, to the Mafia, because my oath to you is all that matters. I've been hiding in a Harvard dorm, a favor from my Old Norse network. I never even taught at Harvard. That's why I thought no one would think to look for me there. Three weeks have passed, and no signs of Ragnarök. It worked. I want my life back. I want you back. It has all been for you."

She was floating, drunk or high, or both. But she had to keep her cool. She needed to think clearly.

"You betrayed me. You lied to me."

"I did. Some. Though for the most part, I didn't tell you things."

"You destroyed the spindle. I was supposed to use it."

"But it worked."

"You're still a criminal as far as the police are concerned."

"I am ready to cooperate. I will go tomorrow and turn myself in. I will cooperate and help them take down the Mafia."

She inhaled. Her heart ached, but it was not soul-shattering grief. It was hope that bloomed among the pieces. Like the world outside, the world saved of Ragnarök, her heart was coming back to life.

"Odin and Thor, I missed you," he whispered.

He wrapped his arms around her, crushed his mouth to hers, and pinned her to the door. Gods, his mouth... Oh, gods, his mouth!

He was kissing her, hungry, needy, possessive. His kiss was a statement. His tongue dipped inside her mouth and brushed against hers in hungry strokes. And her stupid body, just like it had all those weeks ago, responded to him. Lit up like a dry bush from the strike of a match.

Everything else fell away around her but his arms, his hard body, his smell. He was as hot as a hearth, and as hard as a stone. Delirious, she was already wrapping her legs around his waist and her arms around his shoulders, clinging to him like a koala in a tree.

He pulled back, panting. "I love you, Ella. Let me get a room in a hotel. There's one nearby. Please, sweetheart."

He didn't kill Nick. He wasn't in the Mafia. He was Channing, her overprotective, controlling Viking.

And he was alive.

And Ragnarök had ended.

Weeks of terror were over. Whatever he had done, it had worked.

They could have their future.

She knew she shouldn't let him off the hook so easily, and they definitely had a lot to talk about. But all she could say was "Yes."

TWENTY-TWO

He didn't remember how they got to the hotel. It was a block away, a Hyatt perhaps. Earlier today, he'd left his car in a down-town parking garage nearby, not wanting to deal with traffic. He got them a room with a credit card account under a fake name. He'd set it up years ago, just in case someone discovered his secret and he needed to start over...

He'd never imagined using it to escape the Mafia...or woo the love of his life.

As he rushed with her through the beautifully manicured lobby—all muted tones and chrome finishings—her hand was in his, charging him with sweet energy, with desire, with love.

Then they were in the elevator and kissing.

Then the hall, making an awkward, hurried attempt to unlock the room door with the key card...

And then they were finally alone.

As the door shut behind them, he held her in his arms. They were both panting, their foreheads pressed together. He inhaled that fruity, feminine scent of hers.

"You are everything that's good and right about this world," he murmured. "And I love you."

She opened her mouth to say something, but he put his finger against her lips.

"No words now. Not now."

He'd show her with his body instead. He'd show her how much he worshiped her. What she was to him. That she was the part of him that was missing.

The home he'd fought for.

He kissed her. Cupped her face between his hands, drank from her soft, hot mouth as if it were a mountain spring. Her soft breasts pressed into his chest, her heart slammed against him, and his own heart drummed in the same violent rhythm.

Her mouth was sweet and succulent and his.

She was breathing hard, her hands clinging to him, caressing him, digging into the muscles of his shoulders. He picked her up, letting her legs wrap around his waist, and carried her to the bed without stopping the kiss.

He carefully put her on top of the soft duvet cover. Then he pulled away from her and positioned himself between her thighs. She sat right in a spot of sunlight, and her hair was ablaze with golden fire, her skin a smooth, polished stone. There was something eternal and magical about her, and for the first time since he'd known her, he knew she wasn't just human.

She was godlike. Light and pure goodness seeped through her, but there was also more...Norns were the most powerful beings in the world.

And she had power, all right. He could feel it, like the crackling of static electricity before a storm. It was not just that, though. Not just her time-controlling powers. It was also her soul. Wounded and forever loving. The soul of a warrior, just like his.

He undid her trousers and pulled them down her legs, then her shoes. She gasped as he stroked his hand up her thigh, right to her panties, and his cock hardened and jerked, craving her. He wanted her so much, his mouth watered. But he kept going farther up her stomach, under her blouse, brushing the silky skin of her soft belly, and up to her bra. He cupped one of her beautiful breasts, feeling himself swell and his balls tighten. He circled her nipple until she arched her back and tilted her head back, giving out a throaty moan.

"I want to see all of you," he murmured as he rose and pulled her blouse up, and then she was before him in just her underwear.

"Every time we made love or were happy," he murmured, "it was in the darkness, under the pressure of impending doom, under the threat of death. It's only now I can see you, pure and beautiful and whole, bathed in the sun."

He hoped it was the first of many times.

She bit her lip and grinned. "Then I want to see all of you, too."

He chuckled and stood up in front of her. In one movement he pulled up the T-shirt and the hoodie he had on. She sucked her breath in, watching him as he pushed his jeans and briefs down. His erection sprang from them, and her mouth opened, her perfect pink lips swollen as she looked at it, and he got even harder.

Gods, how he wanted those lips around his cock. But not before he pleased her in every way he could imagine.

Like a perfect seductress, she reached around to her back and undid her bra, letting it fall, and her breasts were there with soft, pink nipples he ached to take into his mouth.

Then she pulled down her panties and she was completely naked before him, her skin glowing in the sunlight, her hair like a golden halo around her.

He'd always thought of himself as a Viking, but he wasn't one by blood.

She was the Viking. She even had a battle scar. The bandage on her shoulder got smaller, but was still there.

A Valkyrie. Breathtaking and naked and powerful before him.

He dropped to his knees, spread her thighs, then her soft folds, and sealed her sex with his mouth. She gave out a deep, guttural moan that brought a tremor through his own body as he circled his tongue around, concentrating on her clit. A tremor went through her, too. His left hand was on her inner thigh and caressed it, going up slowly, while his right one was spreading her folds before him.

He licked and teased and pleasured her until she was shaking. His heart was beating in his chest like a war hammer, his pulse threatening to break out of his skin. He inserted two fingers inside her and felt her squeeze him, and as he circled them, she started producing kitten-like moans that went straight into his crotch.

He felt her body tense and her inner walls clench around him, and he knew she was about to come.

He inserted another finger and intensified his movements where he knew it would bring her the most pleasure. She moaned and began moving her pelvis.

She came around him, his golden Viking goddess, milking his fingers with the spasms of her sex. Her cries were urgent, and her pleasure was his, and she was his. And he loved her. Every inch of her.

As his golden goddess quieted, he watched her breathe, pink-cheeked and red-lipped and bright-eyed. And as happy and satisfied as a cat after a bowl of cream.

"Now it's your turn to be in the sun," she murmured as she grabbed his hand and pulled him to her so that he sat down at the edge of the bed, facing her. He was barely aware of the room, but the bedsheets were soft against his skin.

She knelt before him, just like he had before her, and his balls tightened in anticipation.

"Goddess," he whispered. "You don't have to—oh, gods…"

Her mouth was on his cock, those perfect pink lips he'd dreamed of before were on him, and he sank into the velvety, silky pleasure of her tongue and mouth. She caressed his length up and down, and as she cupped his balls, he growled something out that even he didn't recognize.

His fists clenched in the sheets as she teased him, up and down, sucking him, bringing sweet, hot pleasure, spilling fire through his veins. His heart beat, his cock was tight, and there was nothing else but sunlight and her and her mouth and her hands…

Gods, her hands…

And then he knew he was on the verge, but he didn't want to come yet. Didn't want this moment to end. They'd lived through *Fimbulwinter*.

He wanted more of the spring. He wanted more warmth. He wanted eternal sunshine.

He withdrew from her mouth and pulled her up till she was straddling him. He looked into her icy blue eyes, the eyes of a she-wolf, the eyes of a goddess.

The eyes of his love.

"I'm going to take you, sweetheart," he said. "And I'm going to fuck you, and I'm going to make you come."

He kissed her again and then kissed the soft skin of her jaw and her neck and down to her breasts. He sucked in one nipple and nibbled and teased and circled around it. His hand caressed her back up and down and cupped her ass, so round and firm and gorgeous, and soon she was squirming and grinding against him.

Until she found his erection with her hand and sat herself on him.

"The condom…" He groaned as her sweet, tight depths took him in and he rooted himself into her to his balls.

"I don't care about a condom," she said, her voice urgent. "I want to feel you."

The effect was so overwhelming. He had to stay inside her for a bit to get used to the sensations. But she wanted him, and he wanted her, and she began moving on top of him, up and down, milking his cock, spilling a godly pleasure through him.

He hugged her waist, and buried his face between her breasts, and thrust himself up into her, but it quickly became too much. All this need for her—the desperate ache for her body, for her closeness—was finally being satisfied.

And he couldn't hold back.

There, in the sunlight, they were both bathed in their love and the hope for their future. As he pumped in and out, holding her close, he felt their connection as though they were somewhere between times, between destinies, where only he and she existed.

They were both falling through the cloud, rocking on the waves of pleasure, one breath, one thrust, one heartbeat.

Eternal winter was over.

He was bathing with his goddess in eternal sunshine.

TWENTY-THREE

Ella woke up with Channing's scent in her nostrils and a hot, heavy weight wrapped around her. Sunlight was streaming from the large window. A room service tray was on the coffee table, bearing partially eaten food. They'd never managed to finish their dinner, like horny, horny teenagers.

And, for the first time in what felt like forever, she hadn't dreamed of the port engulfed in flames and the dead Vikings and the triumphant Mafia and her holding the sword, about to kill Channing.

Thank God!

She'd never had so much sex in one day...and, well, one night.

She wriggled in Channing's embrace, and he stirred and pulled her closer. His long, silky hair lay on the pillow. She kissed the tip of his nose, and he opened one green eye and a lazy grin spread across his face. He inhaled deeply and nuzzled his face against her shoulder, his beard tickling her skin.

"I had feared for a moment I dreamed of yesterday," he murmured. "But I didn't. You're here."

She gently caressed the side of his face with her knuckles. "I still can't fully believe it's over."

He lay back on the pillow and studied her with a frown. "Ragnarök is over. But what I want to know if you and I...if our breakup is over, too. If you can really forgive me."

Ella climbed out of his embrace and sat up in bed. She pulled her knees to her chest. Did she forgive him? That was a good question. She certainly wanted him. She'd always want him. He was like an obsession, an addiction she couldn't fight.

She also loved him. And she'd always love him. And last night, it was like a crazy celebration, joy at seeing him alive. After being terrified and grief-stricken, thinking that he might have died, to actually see the love of her life, to be able to touch him and talk to him and love him...

"I know you lied to me to stop Ragnarök, I get that. And I know you thought it was for the best. But you still made all the decisions for me. I had thought we were a team, that we made decisions together. But, just like you tend to do, you took control of the situation without consulting me."

He sat up in bed. "You know I lied to you to protect you and your family. I didn't want the Mafia to know about you. That you were a cop, and that you mattered to me. I wanted to keep you safe."

"Yes. But still..." She looked out the window. The building across the street was sunlit and glowing against the brilliant blue sky. A seagull flew past, and for a moment, she had an impression they might be in Greece on a vacation, not in Boston.

"Ella, I am sorry for having deceived you."

"You are sorry," she said softly, "but do you understand why I'm so upset?"

He ran his fingers through his hair. Pink and silver scars,

old and recent, on his chest and shoulders moved. "I understand why you're upset."

"What bothers me is that...you wanted a future together, and so did I. But how can we build a future together if we're not a team? If one of us still thinks they can make all the decisions for us?"

"Ella, this was a special circumstance. It was about life and death, and not just mine and yours."

"But who's to say it won't happen again? And when we have kids..." She trailed off and his grin widened.

"When we have kids?" he asked, light playing in his eyes. "Does that mean you want us to be together?"

She smiled. She wanted what she'd imagined for them to come true. The little ones, part him and part her, running around in a better, safer world.

"I do want that, Channing, yes."

"You've forgiven me?"

"I don't know that I can fully trust you again. And then there's that thing about your criminal charges."

"Like I said, I'll turn myself in. I'll help you guys get the Mafia. You know I'm not a criminal and have no intention of becoming one."

She sighed. "I know. I like this plan. It's the right thing to do."

He cupped her face. "And as to your concern about decisions, I get your point. I really do. It is easier for me to just decide things for you. Because I must protect you. And I know I can. But I also know you can protect yourself. And you can protect our future children. So I swear to you, we will always be a team. I can never lose you like that again. These weeks without you have been the worst days of my life. I can't promise you we won't argue and that I won't be overprotective again.

But I will never deceive you like that and never break your trust again. Please, Ella."

She blinked. His eyes were intense again, dark and shining with determination at her. He was serious. He meant it. She believed him.

She could feel the cracks of pain in her heart starting to heal. She nodded and felt the corners of her lips spreading in a broad grin.

"Okay," she whispered and laid her hand on his.

He grinned. "Okay?"

"Okay."

He kissed her. The kiss was sweet and quick and full of joy. Then he broke it and hurled himself over her, dropping onto one knee before her, still gloriously naked. He had the body of a warrior, with Nordic tattoos running over his bulging muscles, and hard angles, and battle scars. He took her hand in his, his eyes practically glowing, and her heart slammed in her chest.

"Ella O'Connor," he said, and she let out a ragged breath. "I've wanted to marry you for centuries..." She giggled and he grinned. "I love you. I will always love you, and I don't want to spend another moment of my life without you. Will you marry me?"

The onslaught of emotion contracted her lungs. Happiness spilled into her bloodstream like a drug. The truth was, she couldn't imagine a day without him, either, especially not after she'd spent the past several days thinking she may have lost him forever. That showed her like nothing else that she loved him and wanted everything with him.

"Yes," she breathed out, and he picked her up and swept her into his arms, spun her around, and kissed her. Then they spent hours making sweet, gentle love, long and endless. In this, there was everything they both had ever felt and couldn't say. There was hope, and tenderness, and so much love.

Over a late breakfast, Ella picked up her phone to send a text to Dad that she was fine and with Channing. "Damn it, my phone is dead."

"Mine is out, too," he said. "Let me take you shopping, and then I'll take you home."

"I have my car here, you know," she said.

"I'll take you home with your car." He chuckled.

"I have a better idea," she said. "We go to the station and you come clean. That way you'll have the protection of the authorities against the Mafia."

"Okay."

She looked at him, surprised. "Okay? No arguments? No fighting over this?"

"No fighting. We're a team, remember?"

She gave him a peck on his cheek. "A team."

They dressed and checked out and walked out onto the busy downtown street. It still smelled like spring. People passed by them, talking or hurrying somewhere. Homeless people sat at the corners of the buildings, begging for change.

Channing gave ten-dollar bills to every homeless person they passed. She hoped many of these people would soon regain their jobs and homes now that Ragnarök was past. They walked hand in hand through a world that was busy and alive and lit with the sun.

Then Channing stopped in front of a jewelry store. The shop window showed wedding rings, diamond bracelets, and necklaces sparkling through the glass. Through the glass door, she could see the clerk standing over the glass counter and watching them with a smile.

Was this it? Was this true or was it all a dream, her wishful thinking?

Channing winked. She didn't think she'd ever seen him like this. Carefree, relaxed, playful. He was breathtakingly handsome and sexy and all hers. "Which one do you like?" he asked.

They were all stunning, but she felt odd. She'd never wanted anything super expensive. She'd never chased after luxury or money. All she'd ever wanted was for her family to be safe and happy.

"I really don't want anything fancy..." she started, but trailed off.

There, on one of the little white ring cushions, lay a ring of white gold with a light-blue diamond surrounded by small, tasteful white diamonds.

Channing followed her gaze. "You like that one?" he asked softly.

She looked at him. "Don't you think that's almost like the color of my mother's eyes?"

"It's exactly like that color. Let's go get it."

She looked at the ring again. She could see it more clearly without the glare of the sun on the glass. It must have gone behind a cloud. Then something moved in the reflection of the window.

Screams sounded, along with the screeching of metal against metal.

Ella's stomach dropped.

In the reflection, people ran up the street. A huge, breaking wave roared after them. A tsunami.

TWENTY-FOUR

"Get inside!" Channing roared.

He grabbed Ella, who turned around and looked at the approaching wave in shock. He pulled her back, opened the door, and they were inside. The water rushed towards them between the buildings, carrying cars, people, trash cans, and debris. Channing held the door of the store open as nearby people rushed inside.

The jewelry store was only half a mile from the bank of the Boston Main Channel, and there were many buildings between them to slow the wave...

But it was still coming, and the screams and yells were louder, and metal screeched as cars and other objects were dragged over the concrete. And above it all was the roaring sound of the water.

As the last person rushed inside, Channing closed the door. The wave broke as it reached the intersection and flooded the street to the left and right, meeting the streams that washed in from other streets. Water slammed a car into the wall right next to the shop window. Bangs and more screeching metal came from cars crashing against the buildings. Together with take-out containers, plastic bags, dry leaves and branches and debris, water washed people onto the street, followed by a bicycle, an empty baby stroller, and a dog. Sickly, the sun returned from behind the cloud, and light glared, reflecting off the grayish-green water.

"Stay here!" Channing barked at Ella, then hurried to the door of the shop.

"In your dreams!" Ella yelled as she ran after him.

Through the glass door, he could see the water was about three feet high, but it was going down.

"Sir, if you open the door, we'll be flooded!" cried the shop clerk.

Channing glared at the man. "Don't you think the lives of the people outside are more important than saving diamonds and gold?"

The other people murmured. Someone protested, others agreed with him. They weren't his concern. His fiancée was.

"Goddamn it, can you just stay away from trouble for once?"

She shot him an angry glare. "No."

He grinned. "That's why I love you." *Please don't let anything happen to her.*

He opened the door and stepped forward. An icy cold force hit his legs, biting into his knees like a hungry piranha. Ella followed him, and as soon as they were both outside, three men closed the door behind them.

Before them, one person had already managed to stand up, and Ella rushed to the woman, helping her walk towards the jewelry store. A second person, an old man, didn't move.

The water slowly moved back towards the shore. The undertow pulled at his legs, and he stumbled in the water but regained his balance.

He looked back at Ella. The woman lurched from the force of the water, but Ella managed to keep standing.

But the old man was carried back with the undertow, and Channing hurried to him. Glancing back in the direction of the sea, he didn't see any other huge waves coming. Water rushed towards them from the shore in the distance, but the new waves were lower and unlikely to come this far inland.

As he reached the older man, who had regained consciousness, he helped him stand up. Something was darkening the blue sky. From the sea, icy cold wind blew in his face, bringing a chill down into his bone marrow. The first snowflakes landed on his hands, biting him like wasps.

A storm was coming.

"Quick, into the store," he said, guiding the man.

Sirens wailed somewhere behind the buildings in the distance. Metal screeched louder, a series of crashes exploded through the air, and cars moved towards him as the force of the water pulled them towards the sea.

Supporting the older man as they made their way through the rushing water, Channing looked back. Dumpsters, bicycles, motorcycles, mailboxes, garbage, and debris flowed, bumped, crashed into buildings, lampposts, and streetlights.

Chill spread through his veins as he remembered his father reciting the story of Ragnarök.

The sea serpent, Jörmungandr, would wriggle, causing floods. He would go onto the land and the sea would follow...

Odin, Alfather, this wasn't over. Channing was wrong. Ragnarök hadn't stopped with the destruction of the spindle. It had just given them a short reprieve. Enough time to feel safe and comfortable again. Enough time to remember all that they were losing...

The thought crushed him like a boulder, swept him off his feet stronger than the tsunami.

This wasn't over. The world was still coming to an end. Maybe today.

Inside, the store was full of anxious people murmuring and weeping. There was about one inch of water on the floor, and the store clerk, with the help of three men, bailed water with buckets. An argument exploded in one corner, and a woman yelled at another woman, waving her arms angrily.

Channing helped the man he was still supporting to get to the clerk's office. As soon as the old man was sitting with a coat around his shoulders, Channing returned to the front of the store and saw Ella watching a video on someone's cell phone with a look of worry on her face.

"...tsunamis have been registered all along the East Coast of the United States, Mexico, and Canada," said the reporter on the video. "The UK, the western coast of Europe and Africa were all hit with giant waves, as well. A new snowstorm that emerged, the meteorologists are saying, out of thin air, is heading towards New England. It seems the season of bad weather is not over yet, and we can only hope that the cities and towns most affected will withstand another disaster..."

A dark premonition settled in Channing's chest like a boulder.

"It's not over yet, is it?" Ella said.

Channing could only stare into her beautiful icy blue eyes and shake his head.

"With that spindle, I could have done something," she said. "I could have gone back in time and changed something. Now... the reactor... If it's flooded, the core will melt, and then we'll have another Chernobyl on our hands on top of an eternal winter."

Channing's blood chilled. "Fuck." He ran his fingers through his hair. "We have to find another way..."

"We will," she said. With her eyes shining like blue steel,

she was so beautiful. A Valkyrie. "If only we had a golden spindle!"

Realization struck Channing. "But we do."

Ella froze and looked at him. "What?"

"Georgina and Munchie used a small model of the time machine for tests and experiments at first. It's still there, in my office. Leo has it on one of the sideboards."

"Let's go." Ella laid her hand on the shop door to open it. "This has to work. I have to find a way to change the past."

As they stepped into the receding water, Channing thought there was still one last thing he could do to end all of this for sure.

I have to die...

TWENTY-FIVE

Ella switched on the news in Channing's car as they wound their way through the rubble-strewn streets, water spraying from under the car's tires. He had parked it in a parking garage, so it was not damaged. They needed to know how bad it was.

"Last night, the United Nations fell apart in Paris..." said the dry reporter's voice. "In an unprecedented act of violence, the president of Russia called the president of the United States a common thief. Sources state that a unique seventh-generation nuclear reactor was stolen from Russia and discovered in Boston. Russia demands its reactor back and is threatening the US with a full-scale attack, starting with a nuclear assault on Washington, DC."

Ella suppressed a curse.

"Loki's balls," Channing muttered as he turned a corner, barely passing between two crumpled vehicles. "This is just like back in the mead hall, only with presidents."

"And then millions die..." Ella said.

The wipers were frantically clearing the falling snow off

the windshield. The snow was getting thicker. She was exhausted.

The voice on the radio continued. "Unfortunately, the president of the United States responded by slapping the Russian president in the face. After that, it was hard to keep track of the arguments and actions of the presidents. Some leaders managed to walk away, while others lowered themselves to the level of street violence. It was no better than a neighborhood brawl. Russia, allied with Iran and China, are now at war against Europe and the United States..."

As they drove onto Summer Street and through the Seaport District, something caught Ella's eye. Wolves were watching them from between the buildings. With her stomach churning, she pointed at them, and Channing's eyes darkened. He muttered something under his breath.

The radio reporter kept talking. "And although the US president agreed to return the nuclear reactor, it is not clear whether this could truly happen, as the reactor is now, reportedly, in the hands of the Mafia. Meanwhile, other wars are erupting around the world as each country scrambles for medicine, food, and other resources they will need to survive the returning winter and recover from the destruction wrought by the tsunamis. It is estimated that about nine million people died due to—"

Ella switched off the radio. Her eyes burned with angry, unshed tears.

"How do we get inside the port?" she asked.

"I'll get you inside," Channing said. "We'll find a way. Then I'll make sure you're safely in my office. I believe in you."

Warmth spread in her chest, and she laid her hand on his thigh as he drove. "We are a team," she said.

He looked at her, and there was so much warmth and love in his eyes, her heart ached. "We are."

When they arrived at the port, the gate was open and police and FBI cars lined the road in front. No one stopped them as they drove in. Down in front of building Mo5, there were more cars.

"What do you think is going on?" she asked.

Channing drove to the office building and parked. "I think the government is trying to retrieve the reactor to give it back to Russia. I don't think anyone wants a nuclear war."

Signs of the tsunami were even more visible here. Water covered the asphalt, and giant puddles gathered here and there like little lakes. The sea was unruly, waves crashing against the pier, ships rocking. Several lighter ships had been lifted and tossed, smashed against the asphalt. Containers were turned over. The air was thick with the scent of seawater and something chemical.

Down from building Mo5, the sound of guns suddenly filled the air. A helicopter flew overhead, vibrating the air with the power of its rotors.

"Let's hurry," Channing said, and climbed out of the car. He walked around and opened the trunk and took out his sword.

"Do you have your gun?" Channing asked.

"No," she said. "I was off duty."

"Okay," he said. "Just get behind me. I'll get us through to the office."

There was no one at the entry reception desk. Everyone who wasn't at building Mo5 had probably made a run for it when the police and the FBI arrived. Channing and Ella got into the elevator and rode to the sixth floor, where Channing's office was. They leaned back against the wall as the elevator doors opened, just in case.

A rain of bullets exploded right into the middle of the elevator, past Ella and Channing. Her heart raced. She closed her eyes tight. The shooting stopped, and the next moment when she opened them, Channing was gone.

She opened her eyes, and saw him bring his sword down between the Mafia man's neck and shoulder. The man grunted and fell dead. Someone else was shooting at him from around the corner. He ducked behind the reception counter where his secretary, Shelly, had once sat.

Channing reached out, pulled the machine gun over the dead guy's head, and slid it to Ella. She caught it. Their eyes met, and they nodded to each other.

A team. Finally, a team. It took the end of the world to make this happen.

Staying low, she moved to the edge of the reception desk, and when the guy started firing, she ducked and waited. When he stopped, she rose barely above the desk and shot. He yelled and fell and didn't fire again. Channing nodded to her and then at the door to his office. Behind the glass door and wall, the office looked empty.

They ran to the entry, and Channing opened the door.

No one.

Through the two floor-to-ceiling windows, the sky was darkening, and the snow fell harder. There was a lot of shooting between the police cars and the Mafia who were positioned behind building M05. A golden spindle glistened on the sideboard next to several bottles of alcohol.

Five steps and she could take it in her hand.

"I'm going to travel back in time and—"

"And stop the creation of the time machine," Channing finished. "Find me and tell me not to do it, that it will destroy the world."

No amount of fighting would save the situation. It would only get worse. And with the nuclear reactor threatening the existence of millions, not just in Boston but in the whole country, she couldn't just sit back and watch it happen.

And so she had to do something that might mean she'd never see Channing again.

His eyes were intense on her. She grabbed him by the front of his hoodie and pulled him closer. "We'll find each other."

His eyes softened. He drank her face in. "You're my axis, Ella." He pressed his forehead against hers. "The worlds may spin around us and burn and die and be reborn. But I'll always find my way back to you. Through time, through wolves, through ice and fire. Let the spindle spin all it likes."

She chuckled. "I may be the one spinning it."

"I love you, Ella," he whispered into her lips. "You're everything. *Everything.*"

"And you're more, my Viking."

Their kiss was tender and loving, and she wanted to stretch it out for eternity. But she forced herself to pull away, to walk to the spindle.

With shaking hands, she grabbed it, already feeling its power—the vibration, the thickening of the air on her fingertips.

"Three months back in time," she told herself. "I want to go back in time three months ago."

The pleasure coursing through her felt like having the best meal of her life. Every cell in her body said yes to the sensation of holding the golden spindle. It vibrated, it shook, it sang. She was swallowed into the sweet nothingness.

In that darkness, millions of golden threads surrounded her like a cocoon. She could pull the threads and pull herself to them.

She saw all the possibilities. The destinies.

And then she saw the figures in the blue dress, the green dress, and the lilac dress.

They were blond. They all held spindles and stared at her with astonishment.

Two of them screamed angrily at her, waving their arms with their spindles like knives.

The third, the one in the green dress, shielded her, stood between her and the two others.

"Go!" the echo of the woman's voice came, the voice she'd known for the first years of her life. "Go! Now!"

"How?" Ella screamed.

"You need to see it, Ella. See it clearly. See what you want it to be."

Ella shook her head. "What?"

Her mother made a sweeping gesture, her eyes bright, wide. "Threads! Pull the thread. Spin the spindle!"

The two other figures advanced, strangely slow, but their spindles were sharp and they were aiming for her.

"Do it!" Her mother's voice was urgent.

Ella pulled a thread and began spinning.

But she was awkward, and even though her fingers moved and the thread appeared from the spinning, it was wrong. Something was wrong. She was doing something, but she didn't know how to make it deliberate...

The next moment, she woke up. Fresh autumn air played with her hair, bringing the scents of rotten leaves, and sea and wet wood. The houses were made of dark wood, and had thatched roofs, and smoke rose from the smoke holes. Lomdalen.

Someone walked out of the mead hall.

Mia. Her eyes widened as she saw Ella.

What the hell had she done? Why was she in the Viking Age again?

And then she knew.

This was what all those dreams meant. The final battle of Ragnarök for the destiny of the world.

And the Vikings had to be there, fighting for Odin and the gods of Asgard.

TWENTY-SIX

Channing crawled to Ricardo, who was crouching behind one of the police cars. A half circle of about forty police cars, FBI vehicles, and Humvees faced the entrance to building M05. In the receding, milky gray light of the snowfall, Channing could see men in FBI jackets, a SWAT squad, and soldiers in khaki army uniforms.

"What's going on?" Channing asked.

Ricardo glanced in his direction, then pointed the gun at him. "Freeze! What do you mean, what's going on, Hakonson? Why are you here? You're with the fucking Mafia! You're under arrest! Throw your sword on the ground."

Channing muttered a curse and carefully put the sword on the ground and held his hands up.

"I'm not with the Mafia, Sanchez. I'm on your side."

"Yeah, right." Ricardo reached into the back of his trousers and retrieved his handcuffs. "You have the right to remain silent—"

A bullet flew right past his head and he ducked. So did Channing.

"Look. Can we do this later? I joined the Mafia to get close enough to destroy the time machine, which I did. Now they're trying to kill me, but I've come to help you."

Ricardo shook his head. More bullets flew into the bumper, right next to him. "You're a moron, that's what you are."

"You have to believe me. We're on the same side. We're on Ella's side. We're on the side that wants to stop the Mafia and bring peace. I was going to turn myself in today, anyway, cooperate with you guys and the FBI to get the Mafia behind bars. Let's just get through this and stop them, then you can arrest me all you like."

Ricardo groaned. "And I'm going to be a fucking idiot. The reactor is our top priority, or I'd be arresting your ass right now."

Another bullet pinged against the car, three inches away from his head. Ricardo ducked his head for a moment, then rose and shot back. Channing picked up his sword.

"And put your fucking sword away," growled Ricardo.

"No. I'll need it. Why is Leo holding on to the reactor, anyway?" asked Channing.

"They have a new buyer for the reactor. North Korea."

"Shit."

"Yeah. Shit. And now Russia is making threats, as you might have heard. That's why the FBI and the military are here. It's a matter of national security. Not only could the tsunami have damaged it, but if we don't give the reactor back, Russia is going to nuke us."

Channing groaned. How had he not thought about the ramifications of his actions? Why had he thought he could just buy a nuclear reactor and travel through time without causing upheaval? Yes, he had been desperate to return home, to save his family, but he was still astounded at his own arrogance.

Ricardo's gaze was merciless. "This is all your fault, you realize that, right? You smuggled the damn thing in."

Channing nodded solemnly. It *was* all his fault. If only he could undo it all.

Through the falling snow he looked back at the office building where, a few minutes earlier, Ella had disappeared as soon as she touched the spindle.

"Come on, Ella," he muttered. "You can do it."

"What?" Ricardo followed his gaze. "Is Ella there? Didn't you two break up?" His voice had an edge as sharp as Channing's blade.

"She was. She took the little golden spindle, the model for the time machine, and traveled in time to stop all this."

Ricardo groaned. "And you let her do that? What if she gets kidnapped by that Viking king again?"

Channing gripped his sword tighter. "Let her? Have you met Ella? Anyway, I know she can handle herself. I trust her. You need to do that, too."

Despite his words, the slightest thought of Ella being harmed tore at Channing's heart.

"What's the plan here, with the Mafia?" he asked.

"The plan is to stop the enemy and to get the reactor without making a nuclear wasteland out of Boston."

The sky darkened, and the wind grew stronger. Black storm clouds blew in from the sea. Snow whirled in short, rapid blows and then long, powerful gusts. Waves crashed against the pier, uncharacteristically high, and the ships that were docked at the port rose and fell. The screech of metal against metal and concrete tore the air.

Channing blinked against the snow. He hoped Ella was okay, that she was able to control her powers with the spindle. Because there wasn't much time left to act.

Distantly, thunder boomed right in the middle of a black

storm cloud.

A verse from the legend of Ragnarök came to mind.

THE WORLD TREE *Yggdrasil shudders and groans...*

The Midgard serpent Jörmungandr furiously writhes, causing waves to crash.

A CALL of an eagle came from somewhere, then another...

Icy dread descended over Channing as he saw wolves— hundreds of them—sprint towards him through the snow, like an army ready to listen to their commander.

He needed to get them away from the police and the FBI, or the wolves might start attacking them. Staying low, he sprinted away from Ricardo, towards the angry sea.

But he'd managed to get only about thirty feet away from the last line of cars when the gates to building Mo5 opened. Channing watched as a crane moved forward, carrying the nuclear reactor.

Leo Esposito's voice came over a loudspeaker from inside of the warehouse. "Get out of our port or I will blow up the reactor. I will throw a grenade in there and blow it up! Leave!"

Gods, Ella had been right all along. Fighting wouldn't change anything because he wasn't fighting for the right side.

Despite his best intentions in trying to prevent Ragnarök, he'd been fighting on the side of chaos all along. Ricardo was right. The nuclear reactor was his doing. Had he used his wealth for less selfish reasons, he could have done more to help the planet, to help the poor, to help abused women...something his mother would have been proud of and maybe even bene- fited from.

As the wolves gathered around him, sitting and waiting, he

knew what this was.

The last battle. The battle for the destiny of the world.

"Sit!" he yelled at the wolves, hoping they would listen to him like dogs would. They barely glanced at him, their ears upright in the direction of the police, the FBI, and the army.

Ricardo looked back at him and froze, astonishment and fear in his eyes. He pointed his gun at the wolves. They growled. Like a wave, the wolves ran at the police. Ricardo started firing his gun, and, alerted, the other cops did, too. Two waves of humans and wolves clashed.

Goddamn it!

Someone reached him and drove a fist into Channing's face. Channing hit him back. One of the Mafia men.

He didn't want to kill anyone. He just had to stop Leo, stop the wolves if he could.

Then a man in a beanie, holding a machine gun, climbed on top of an SUV. It was Clicker, Channing realized. With a wild grin, he directed his machine gun into the fight between the military forces and the wolves. People fell and didn't move.

Channing held his sword, panting, unable to believe what was happening before his eyes. The wolves were jumping at the police and the FBI and the military, teeth gnashing at their throats. The Mafia were shooting at the distracted authorities.

One of SWAT officers managed to get free of the wolf attacking him and shot Clicker, and he toppled from the car.

As more police and military fell, the Mafia men broke through their line and came at Channing. But the wolves ran at them, too, protecting him. The animals whimpered and growled, tearing throats apart, biting into flesh like furry lightning bolts. People beat them back. Gunshots rang out. Screams and yells sounded through the snowy insanity.

Blood and bodies covered the ground.

This was the end.

TWENTY-SEVEN

Mia gasped and ran to Ella. "Ella, what's going on?"

"The final battle has come. It has come."

People walked onto the streets from the houses. From the mead hall, Hakon strode towards them, his shoulder in a sling. John and the younger Mia followed him. Ella's eyes filled with tears of joy at seeing them. At seeing Hakon alive. Channing would be so relieved to know his father had survived being shot by King Harald.

"What is going on?" Hakon's voice boomed as he hurried down the slope to Ella.

"I didn't intend to come here," Ella said. "The final battle of Ragnarök has started back in the twenty-first century and our last hope was for me to change the past. But I ended up here instead of stopping Channing from creating the time machine."

"The final battle?" asked Hakon. He looked a little pale, but he held his head and shoulders high and proud. "And Ulf?"

"He's alive."

"Thank the gods," muttered John. "Father, we must go there to fight for Odin at the last battle of Ragnarök."

Ella shook her head, though she somehow understood this was why she was here. "They have guns. What can your axes and swords do? It's suicide."

Mia nodded. "She's right. There's nothing you can do."

"And yet," said a voice behind Hakon, and they all turned to see who it was. "Young John is right. It is Ragnarök. And the place of Norse warriors is there."

The Norns. All three of them stood together. They were old again, white hair in Nordic braids around their heads. Eternal eyes watching everyone coolly. Golden spindles glistening in their hands.

Ella's blood chilled.

Her mother was looking straight at her. Only, she wasn't her mother now, she was the Norn. An eternal being that defined cruel destinies. An eternal being that had sentenced Channing and the world to death.

"No," Ella said, hoping there was some other way even still. "This is not the plan. They can't do anything against guns and grenades. They'll all die."

The three Norns looked at her, and Ella thought she saw cold fury blazing in the eyes of her two aunts. Her mother gave her a sad smile.

"It is their destiny," said the Norn in the blue dress. "It has been woven and no one can change it."

"Ragnarök has come," said the one in the lilac dress. "The place of every Norse warrior is on the battlefield with their swords and axes, fighting for the gods."

This would mean her dream would come true. Her apocalyptic dream with the dead Vikings and the world burning and Channing dying by her hand.

"No!" she cried.

Hakon looked at Ella. "It is truth. I will go and help my son, even if my place is to die by his side."

Mia shook her head, tears in her eyes. "No, Hakon. Please."

"Sweet, this is the way of a Viking. I love you, and I know I will come back to you."

She clung to him. "You say that every time you go to battle."

"And I have come back to you every time. I will return to you again."

The warriors who gathered around him raised their swords and axes and roared a battle cry.

"As long as Ulf Hakonson lives," said her mother sadly, "the world will die. Go to your ships, brave warriors. It is time to set sail to the battle for the destiny of the world."

Before Ella could say anything more, the Vikings ran down the slope onto the jetties and climbed into their dragonships. She ran after them, her mind full of images of the dark skies and the burning sea, and the ash raining down, and the dragon-ships rocking on the waves, going with full sails towards the Port of Boston.

And then the Norns spun their spindles, and the world became a net of golden threads, and then everything went dark.

AMID THE CRASHING waves and the darkness, Channing saw a sail...two...three sails... He blinked, not trusting his vision. Viking sails, just like his father's dragonships, with long figure-heads of dragons on the hulls. They were rocking on the waves, coming towards the port.

Channing stared in shock as he saw, on the closest ship, Ella standing at the bow, hugging the dragon's head.

Next to her, holding his sword and his ax, a fur cloak on his shoulders, was Hakon. Next to him was his sister, Mia, and his brother, John.

No, no, no!

She wasn't supposed to have done that. She was supposed to have changed the past!

He pushed away one of the Mafia goons who came at him and ran towards the ships. The police were clearly losing, and no reinforcement came. As if in a dream, the ships docked despite the big waves, and Channing tied the lines to the cleat. The ramps were lowered, and Viking warriors spilled into modern-day Boston.

Ella ran to Channing and fell into his hug. "You're alive," she whispered against his lips, half kissing, half talking. "You're alive."

"You, too!" he whispered, pressing her into his arms. "What did you do?"

Hakon came to him, big and tall and wide as an ox, and Channing hugged him. Hakon returned a few taps on his back. Three dozen or so wolves behind them separated from the pack and came growling at the Viking.

"You shouldn't have come," said Channing. "Are you all right?"

"I am fine. Your mother patched me up. I will never leave you in trouble, son."

He wasn't fine, Channing could see that. He was paler, and he held his weapon in his other hand.

"And you two." Channing looked at his brother and sister. "Why the hell are you two here?"

"This is Ragnarök, brother," said John.

"Do you think a true Norseman or woman would sit back and let others die while Odin needs us?" Mia said proudly.

"I landed there by accident," said Ella. "I didn't mean to. I still don't know how to control my powers. And then the Norns were there, and they sent everyone here. Said it's their destiny to fight in the final battle."

"We had to come, son," said Hakon.

There were about four hundred Vikings from the three ships combined, and the first battle with the wolves began.

But at the same time, the Mafia had pushed back the wolf-besieged law enforcement and military, and seeing the odd men with swords and axes and shields, Mafia goons started firing the first shots.

A helicopter droned somewhere, coming closer, and more police sirens sounded nearby, getting louder.

In a few moments, the port was a battlefield. Channing wielded his sword left and right, fighting the Mafia. Ella found a gun that someone had dropped and shot into the wolves. Hakon was fighting, too, like a massive warrior from the legends, but his movements were accompanied by a mask of pain.

It was getting darker, though it still couldn't be much past noon. The ground shook, and the fight stopped as men and beasts lost balance. Waves grew, each higher than the one before, until a giant wave rose like a wall. It lifted the ships and drove them forward into the port. One of them crashed into the container crane, and it fell with an earth-shuddering tremor, crushing police officers, wolves, and Vikings beneath it.

Icy cold water swept over them all, driving people and beasts under its surface. Channing lost his balance from the power of the wave and was thrown into the snow. Ella held on to one of the cars.

And then, in the darkness that was the sea, an explosion came, and a tower of flame shot into the air. Channing froze, blinking.

Flames spread across the sea, and the next wave didn't bring water.

It brought fire.

A chemical smell spread, the acrid smell of death. Rolling waves of fire rushed into the port.

Like a flagship, an overturned, burning tanker rolled right on top of the wave. Flames lit the white upside-down letters *SURTR*.

The flames spread onto the boats and the surrounding buildings, turning the world from ice to fire. Another wave surged, and a forklift rose like a burning giant and came crashing into one of the warehouses.

Odin, the reactor!

TWENTY-EIGHT

Ella scrambled to her feet, blinking away the freezing seawater mixed with snow. The sea was burning; the snow was burning, the fire spreading through the frozen ground as if it were paper. It was consuming the bodies of wolves and people, and the scent of burning hair and flesh stank.

It was her dream, her nightmare come true.

Channing... Where was he?

The sky was pitch-black. The electricity was out, but the flames illuminated everything in a blinding inferno.

The sun became black... She remembered the verse from *The Poetic Edda*.

Another fire-wave crashed into the ships and the pier, but it was smaller than the previous one, and it threw only droplets of fire.

The remaining wolves attacked again, fangs flashing. Some of them were on fire, but they kept attacking, spreading the flames to their victims.

The helicopter above was buffeted by the strong wind,

snow, and flames and fell, swinging in circles, into the burning sea.

The high-pitched sirens of fire engines grew louder and closer.

Thank God, she thought as she trembled and shook from the cold. If they didn't burn to death or get eaten by wolves, they'd all die soon of hypothermia.

But as gunfire exploded next to her, she knew she may die from a bullet sooner.

She picked up her gun with shaking hands, and saw the fire crawling closer to the nuclear reactor. Leo Esposito stood atop the fallen forklift, grinning wildly at the chaos in front of him. Someone sitting in the crane that held the nuclear reactor was slowly putting it down.

"You thought I wouldn't kill you, you bastard? I'll kill you and everyone that's dear to you!"

She knew he was talking to Channing. The man must be mad.

Channing swung his sword against a man who held a gun at him. He knocked the gun out of the man's hands and it flew away. The man picked up a piece of burning wooden debris and shoved it at Channing. Channing slashed across, cutting off the top part of the board.

Hakon was fighting the wolves right next to him. Why were they attacking the Vikings when they were on Channing's side?

Because the Vikings were here to stop Ragnarök, she knew. Because they were on Odin's side.

And Ragnarök was the doing of giants like Surtr, and of Channing.

John wielded his ax, protecting himself from the wolves. Mia was by his side, slashing with her scramasax.

Another earthquake shook the ground. Cracks ran under Ella's feet, and the cars and the ships moved. Hakon lost his balance and missed cutting off a wolf's head. The beast used that moment to jump on Hakon's chest and bite into his neck. Ella yelled, raised her gun, and shot. The wolf was knocked back and fell to the ground with a whimper of death.

She ran to Hakon, but two more wolves jumped on top of him, whimpering from the fire that was consuming their pelts, and bit into him. Hakon didn't cry out, just jerked and hit one of the wolves over and over with his sword. Another wolf attacked, but John stepped in to fight it off.

Ella fired and got one. Mia stabbed the other one with her scramasax, but more came at her, attacking, and she turned around, slashing her scramasax against them.

Hakon rose, swaying. Blood dripped down his neck and shoulders. A giant black shadow appeared between the wolves. As giant as a bear, with silvery eyes. Head low, teeth bared, as long and sharp as knives. The low growl that came from the beast was audible even through the screams of the fighting crowd, the gunshots, the roar of fire, and the yapping of the wolves.

Fenrir.

The beast that would kill Odin and swallow the sun.

The beast that had saved Channing once.

The beast that was Ragnarök itself.

She fired and missed.

Hakon raised his sword, but slowly. Fenrir launched himself at Hakon in a black wind of fur and teeth.

Ella shot again, and Hakon slashed at the wolf with his sword, but his stroke was too early. He must have lost a lot of blood and was wounded badly. Fenrir's teeth flashed and sank into Hakon's neck. Ella's next bullet hit the wolf in the shoulder, but he didn't move. Hakon screamed as the wolf raised its head at her and growled, blood trickling from its bared fangs. She fired again.

Right into the bastard's head, right between the eyes. Fenrir whimpered like a pup, and fell in a heap of fur.

With her feet and hands icy cold from fear, she ran and dropped to her knees by Hakon's side.

Hakon was unrecognizable.

PAIN LANCED through Channing's heart when he saw his father. His face was a raw, bloody mess. His neck was torn and blood pumped out in quick bursts.

"No!" Channing yelled.

John and Mia dropped to their knees by their father's side.

"Children," Father gurgled, "honor...to die...by your side... Valkyries already..."

Channing's vision blurred. He knew what Hakon meant. He'd died in a battle, the honorable way for a Viking. He'd go to Valhalla.

Like Odin himself, who'd died when Fenrir had swallowed him.

Only, like everything, this was Channing's fault.

He looked at Ella. "You must go back in time and change this, Ella. Please."

Around them, Vikings were dying—shot, ravaged by wolves. Fire consumed wolves and people alike. One fire engine was shooting foam into the flames, but the other two now lay on their sides, burning.

Most of the police and the FBI lay dead, as well as the Vikings. The military was still shooting at the Mafia. This was a sick massacre.

And despite the firefighters' efforts, the flames crept ever closer to the nuclear reactor, which now stood on the floor of building M05.

Was it all worth it? Hundreds had died today, including his father, including his sword-brothers.

Someone ran at Ella, another Mafia guy.

She rose to her feet and fired, but the gun clicked without a shot. Channing moved to protect her, but she delivered a kick into the goon's stomach that threw him back.

Before he could go and throw the guy off her, everything stilled. There was a great flash of golden light that froze and illuminated everything as though someone had pressed pause.

In the center of the battle, King Harald appeared. His beard was fiery red in the golden light, and he was wearing a rich *brynja* and held a giant battle ax with intricate Nordic patterns on its shiny surface. Three old ladies with hair as white as cotton grass stood around him. They were dressed in green, blue, and lilac.

Then it all resumed as though nothing had happened. He blinked, and King Harald stood before him.

Channing shot a glance at Ella. She hadn't seen the king yet, and she punched the man who was attacking her in the nose.

She had a handle on it.

"Harald," Channing said, gripping his sword.

"Do you see everything around you? Do you now believe that you are the end of the world?"

Channing did. Of course he did. He saw the fire only inches away from the nuclear reactor. Boston would be destroyed.

And the rest of the world would follow.

The man Ella was fighting got a hold of a gun and she was weaponless.

He had fought so long and hard for his own happiness.

Fighting was his way of life. That was how he'd been

brought up. That was how he'd spent all fourteen years of his life here in the twenty-first century.

Fighting against destiny. Fighting against time. Fighting against himself.

He'd found the greatest happiness of his life. The woman he loved. The woman who made him feel like he was home, after thirty-two years of being in exile from himself. She was the one, the only one.

The only thing that mattered.

And if he didn't do what he should have done right away, she'd die.

Not just her.

Billions of people. This was the end of the world.

He was out of options. There was only one thing he could do.

Channing raised his sword, nodded, and slashed. Harald grinned and lifted his ax, meeting Channing's blade. The guy fighting Ella had the gun in his hand and she grabbed it, forcing it up. He shot wildly one, two, three times.

Harald swung the ax in a great horizontal line, aiming for Channing's stomach. *Just don't move. Just let the ax take you.*

He stepped back, letting the ax slide past.

Leo threw a grenade into the reactor.

The man fighting Ella pushed his gun down and aimed right at her face.

Harald swung the ax towards Channing's neck.

Just don't move. Just let it take you.

He dropped his sword.

I love you, Ella.

TWENTY-NINE

When he opened his eyes, he was warm. There was no icy cold wind or fire burning his face, he was just...

Fine.

No ache in the old wounds, no pain in the new ones. His muscles weren't tired. He breathed easy.

Well-being washed through him.

He felt like a newborn baby.

The blurry gold and green colors sharpened into a landscape before him, and he blinked.

He was in Boston, in Christopher Columbus Park, lying on the soft green grass. The sun shone, and there was a gentle breeze. Seagulls squawked high above.

He propped himself up on his elbows. In front of him, with a backdrop of skyscrapers and tall buildings, was his father's mead hall from Lomdalen.

Someone stood at the large entrance gate, an old man with a long, shaggy beard and an eye patch. Channing recognized him from his trip to the Viking Age. The man who had helped him in the forest. Odin, he understood with sudden clarity. How had he not seen it before?

"There you are," Odin said and gestured for Channing to come in. "My hero."

Channing stood up, his head pleasantly void, his chest calm.

Ella, he remembered. And a pang of pain shot right through his heart.

"Drink this," Odin said and gave him a horn that smelled like honey. "Mead. The drink of gods."

Channing took the horn and sipped. Delicious. The pain in his heart melted away and the peaceful numbness returned.

He entered the hall, and it was just like he remembered, the central hearths in the middle, the tables and benches, the great table of honor for the jarl and his wife. Alcoves, one of which he'd used with Ella.

Pain returned, twisting and cutting within him like barbed wire. He drank more of mead, and it went away.

"Is this Valhalla?" He turned to Odin.

"It is."

"Did it work?"

"What?"

He swallowed. "I died. Did it stop Ragnarök?"

Odin pulled a horn of mead out of thin air and drank. "It did."

Channing sighed out. He should have done it earlier, then no one would have had to die. So many had died...including his father.

"Is Ella all right?"

"She is."

"And Boston?"

"More fire engines came and extinguished the fire. The sea calmed. The snowstorm went away. The wolves left. More military troops came and put the end to the Mafia. Ella lives. The world goes on."

Ella lives...without him.

The thought was like a stab. He drank more mead, and so did Odin. Numbness returned, his head spinning pleasantly.

"Why me?" he asked. "Why was I the reason for the end of the world?"

Odin took a deep breath and exhaled before he walked to one of the columns. He moved his hand, and the carvings changed. Three figures spinning spindles under the world tree Yggdrasil moved their hands. Golden threads formed from under their spindles, reminding him of the threads that his time machine made.

"The Norns are the most powerful creatures in the world, you see. Even the gods, we are slaves to whatever they decide our destiny will be.

"Your mother made a deal for you with one of them.

"Your destiny was to go back to your own time. You were not supposed to defy them. You were supposed to accept your destiny. But you did not. Every human's desire is to make their own destiny.

"When you chose to stay in the past, it disrupted the balance of time.

"You were sent to the twenty-first century to regain that balance because your place is there.

"And yet still, you used science and technology to bend destiny to your will. The worst thing was it worked. Your destiny changed, and you angered the Norns further. Norns define destiny before people are born. They cannot change it, and you did with your time machine.

"As a human, it is your nature to fight for things and want things and get things.

"It is the same thing you humans do with nature. You abuse

the world around you to selfishly take what you like, and for what? Power. Riches. Your own importance.

"And yet, one of the Norns fell in love with a human. Skuld, Ella's mother.

"She saw the destiny of her daughter. And that destiny was you.

"Just like there is no one else like you, there is no one else like Ella. You were born between times. She was born between a human and a Norn.

"You tore the world apart, and she has the power to heal that tear. Where you were the power of destruction, she is the power of healing."

Channing drank more.

"So I brought it on myself."

"You did. The whole of humanity did. You're just an example."

Channing sat on the bench next to Odin. "I always thought once I had enough time and money, I'd make a big difference in the world. I'd support environmental initiatives, I'd implement the latest green energy technology in the port, use wind and solar energy. I always thought, once I became even richer, I could do this. I should have tried harder. I should have made a real difference."

"Perhaps. Did you not have enough riches to do that already?"

Channing drank more mead. "I did, Alfather. I did. I could have made a positive difference. I could have stopped and appreciated what I had, what I could do for the world, instead of selfishly pursuing the home I lost and perhaps never truly had."

"So, was it about home?"

"Yes. I don't think I ever felt truly at home in the Viking Age. But it was the only home I knew. The warmth of my family. Their love. The friendship of the community. And yet, I didn't feel at home in the twenty-first century, either. The only time I felt at home was with Ella. She was my home. And with her, the twenty-first century could become one."

"But now, here we are. The sacrifice has been made. I gave my eye for wisdom. You gave something, too."

"My life."

"What did you give it for?"

Channing thought about it. The regret of seeing the world go on without him was as sharp as jealousy. Watching the rest of the world live, laugh, cry, make mistakes...be with their loved ones...everyone but him.

He'd never be with Ella. He'd never hold their child. He'd never whisper how much he loved her, how much of a miracle she was to him. He'd never kiss her and make love to her.

What had he done it for?

He knew he was wrong to hold on to the selfish need to be happy with her when the whole world suffered because of him.

He had sacrificed himself for her.

He had done it for the people of the world, across all ages.

He had done it so that humanity could learn to be better.

He raised his horn of mead as pain tore his chest apart at the thought of Ella. But this time he didn't drink. He let the pain flow through him, and he welcomed it as a reminder of those he'd lost. "As much as I want to say it was for eternity with you, Odin...I did it for love."

THIRTY

One week later...

"HONEY, WE HAVE TO BURY HIM." Dad's quiet voice was like thunder and Ella shuddered.

Channing's apartment was silent. The fire didn't play in the broken hearth-like fireplace. Nothing beeped or ticked. The electronic clock on the damaged oven didn't glow, and no lights were on.

Outside the floor-to-ceiling window, Boston lived and moved, golden in the sunlight. Lines of cars flowed through the streets, and tiny people moved about, looking like ants from this height. Puffy white clouds soared in the blue sky.

There were no signs of snow. No wolves. No Mafia.

No Channing.

Something within the emptiness inside her made the muscles in her throat move and produce "I know."

Dad rolled his wheelchair closer and took her hand in his,

warm and reassuring. "He saved the world. He did the right thing."

Tears welled in her eyes, and the dusty hardwood floor blurred. "I know."

Her chest hurt. She wasn't breathing. If she breathed, the hole in the middle of her chest would tear her apart, send agony burning through her veins.

Oblivion. Numbness. That was what she needed.

Drink.

She took her hand away from her dad's and walked to Channing's liquor cabinet. The glass door had been broken, as well as most of the bottles. Surprisingly, a single bottle of scotch remained in the far corner.

"You're driving, hon," Dad said softly.

Damn it.

She gently set the bottle on the granite countertop of the kitchen island. "I know."

He looked around. "Where would his property deeds be?"

"Upstairs, in his office. I'll look for them in a minute."

She needed the deeds to deal with this place. But what was she going to do with everything?

In his will, he'd left all of his property, all of his belongings, all of his wealth to her. But she didn't need any of it. This apartment, without him, was a raw, corroding wound. The cars, she couldn't even look at them. She hadn't signed any papers. Signing them would make it final. Would make his death real, just like burying him.

The port...

The port was the only thing that she could stand, the only place where she felt relief. Strange, since hundreds of people had died that day, and it was considered dangerous to go there because of the radiation that had leaked from the reactor. Thank God the grenade hadn't actually gone off, or the whole city would have had to be evacuated. It turned out Leo hadn't pulled the pin. Either he was too out of his mind to do it properly, or he didn't actually want to die.

Despite all that, the port called to her. It was the last place she'd seen Channing alive.

She'd seen that moment, the moment the ax was heading for his neck, and he'd stood there. He'd closed his eyes, his face resolved.

Even peaceful.

Someone had shot the man who attacked her, or she'd be dead, too. The next moment, as though by magic, the clouds had dissipated, the snow had stopped falling, and the black sun had returned to normal.

Wolves had run away.

The Norns had sent the Vikings back to their time, where they were supposed to be.

The police, the feds, and the military sent reinforcements and arrested the remaining Mafia.

Everyone's world had gone back to normal.

Only hers had ended.

"He saved me, Dad," she said, running her hand along the granite countertop. "He saved you and Gloria. He saved Ted. He saved everyone."

"He did."

A sharp pain shot through her like a spear and she doubled up. "What am I going to do without him? I should have spent every minute appreciating him. He was right. We only had a limited time. What am I going to do?"

Dad rolled his wheelchair next to her and laid his hand on her back. "You are going to live. It will hurt. For a while. Maybe your grief will never be completely gone. But you will keep living."

She straightened up and wiped her tears. "I don't want to."

Dad's face hardened and his eyes widened in fear. "No, Ella, honey, don't you dare think that."

"You just don't understand."

———

LATER, in her room, Ella took out her mom's embroidery. The linen fabric, the colored threads, and the needle.

She'd do what she had failed to do. She had told Channing she'd go to another time and change things.

She was still a Norn—the daughter of one, anyway. Channing had sacrificed his life for the good of the world. She needed to make a sacrifice, too. She refused to believe that a world without Channing was worth it. She'd create a new destiny. She had to try, at least.

Taking the golden spindle and a piece of fresh wool that was left among some of her mother's things, she began spinning. She didn't know how; she'd never spun yarn in her life, only seen her mother do it and the women in the Viking Age. Even though it was hard at first, somehow, her hands knew what to do, and she didn't stop. Perhaps it was in her blood, just like the völva had said. That wisdom, that power she still was not able to fully control...

Somehow, she knew it was because of her lack of trust. She hadn't fully trusted Channing, even though he had told her the truth. Everything he had done was to protect her.

And she didn't trust herself.

Too bad. Because look at her hands, spinning, holding the spindle at the correct angle, dropping it with the right strength, holding the yarn just so. She was stronger and more powerful than she'd thought. She was wiser.

She knew what to do, if she only trusted herself.

Vikings always sacrificed something to please the gods, to gain their favor.

That was what she'd do, too.

In the early hours of the morning, when she had a good amount of yarn, she took her mother's needle, put the yarn through the eye, and began working on an embroidery. She lost the feel for what was real and what she dreamed. She entered that state of mind that she had in her dreams when she could change things. Reality blurred. The borders between what was real and what was possible softened.

All that mattered was the destiny she was creating on the tapestry in front of her.

It would be the last and the best thing she'd ever do as a half Norn. This would be her sacrifice.

Her powers. Her magic.

She wouldn't be a Norn anymore. She wouldn't be able to change time.

She remembered her mother's words. *You need to see it, Ella. See it clearly. See what you want it to be.*

That would be how she'd change the world. She'd see what she wanted, exactly and precisely.

She saw a different time, a different reality where everything would be better. And even though she'd told Channing he shouldn't deal with problems by traveling through time, she was doing just that. But she understood his desire better now. Just as he was searching for his home, she was searching for hers.

She didn't know how much time passed until, finally, the tapestry was ready. It glimmered with golden and silver threads, even though she hadn't dyed the yarn, and there on the tapestry was the better world she envisioned, with a better her...and him.

Alive.

She looked around. She was no longer in her room but stood in a vast darkness, just like when she'd seen the Norns before.

And then one of them stood right in front of her. Golden hair. Green dress. Blue eyes. She wasn't a young woman like the last time Ella had seen her in this space. She was a sweet old lady with a spindle in her hand.

Ella swallowed. "Mother."

The Norn smiled. "Hello, sweetheart."

"Where am I?"

"You are in between, dear. In between worlds, times, destinies. When I help people travel in time, they pass this place quickly. But you and I can stop here. Here, things have not happened yet. Here, you can change things."

"Why are you here?"

Skuld cocked her head and took two steps. "I wanted to see you for one last time, and I want to explain what you are actually about to do and see if you are sure."

"Okay."

"Although I have never taught you anything, you did everything right. You found out everything by yourself. There is no one like you. You are not quite a Norn like me and my sisters, and you are not quite human. You cannot truly define destinies like we do, but you can travel through time and change single events. My sisters were livid with me when I decided to be with your father. They pretty much disowned me...only it does not work like that. I knew it would never last, what your dad and I had. And I never expected to become pregnant like a regular human. But you have to understand. Our lives as Norns are lonely. There are only three of us. All we can do is to watch you humans. Never participate. We do not live. We just exist. And with you and your dad, I lived. Even if only for a few years, I lived. I was happy for the first time in my life."

Ella felt a tear roll down her cheek. "You didn't want to leave me?"

The Norn came closer and took Ella's hand in hers. "Never. Ever."

"Then why?"

"Because the world needed me to do my job. But I protected you. I saw you would love Ulf Hakonson, and that he would love you. And that you would be the one who would heal the tear in reality and create a better world."

She let go of Ella's hand and took her tapestry. "This is the healing, sweetheart. This is exactly the right thing to do."

Ella blinked. "Why?"

"The world now has a huge scar from Ragnarök. It was left by Channing and his time machine, which tore into the balance of time and destiny. With this scar, the world can go on, but will never completely heal. What you wove here...this is healing."

She looked at Ella and pointed at the embroidery. "Here, everyone who died because of Ragnarok will return, as if the events of Ragnarök had never happened. But as you know, there is a price to be paid."

"What is the price?"

"Channing cannot remember who he was. He cannot want to create the time machine again. He will not remember you. He will not remember his roots. He will not remember Ragnarök."

"He won't remember me... How will we ever be together again?"

"That is not all, sweetheart. You will not have your powers anymore. You will not know who I am. And you will not remember him, either."

Shock washed over her, cold and icy.

"But—"

"That is the sacrifice, I am afraid. This is what you wove. And you will need to imagine it very well. Do you still want to do this?"

Ella blinked back the tears that wanted to fall. He'd be alive. He'd be somewhere living in the world. That would be enough.

"Yes," she said, "I do."

"Good. Then do it. I cannot change destiny that has already been woven, nor can my sisters. Whatever we embroidered before the person was born will happen. That was why I had to write the formula for Munchie and Georgina, so that Channing's time machine would work. Although he acted against us Norns, it needed to happen. The world needed to be broken so that it could be healed, made even better." She stroked a bent finger across Ella's embroidery, then cupped her face with one hand. "Men want to change destiny, but they can't change what has been defined by us. The only one who can change what has been woven is you. Half human, half Norn. There is no one else like you. You are the only one who can heal the world."

There was so much adoration and love in her mother's voice that, for the first time, being like no one else didn't sound like a bad thing. It didn't mean being lonely and abandoned.

It meant she could help people. It meant she could make the future that humanity, as well as she and Channing, deserved.

Mom smiled. "Just know one thing before I go. I did not know what love was. Your dad and you taught me to love. You were worth everything."

Something within Ella warmed, as though a small ember was breathed into life right at the center of her being. Her sadness and loneliness melted away. Her inner wound was healing.

And from that healing, she knew she was becoming whole. And she could see the new tapestry even better now. She added more details. She added smiles. She added that warm, glowing ember that would never be extinguished in people's hearts.

The tapestry before her was bright with colors. The city of Boston was calm and peaceful and lush with green trees, flowers, and sunlight. People walked, sat in cafés, rode bikes, and played with children. It was safe and calm and abundant. There were solar panels on the roofs and wind turbines in the sea, and recycling bins on the streets.

And in the middle of it all stood a couple, embracing each other, their foreheads pressed together, looking deep into each other's eyes. She was blond, and he had long hair and Nordic tattoos. Even if they would forget each other, she could include this wish, this final hope in her tapestry.

You're my axis, Ella. The worlds may spin around us and burn and die and be reborn. But I'll always find my way back to you. Through time, through wolves, through ice and fire. Let the spindle spin all it likes...

Was it too much to hope that her noble, brave Viking truly would find her again one day?

THIRTY-ONE

Mo's was busy.

October had turned out to be a pretty peaceful month, apart from the regular misdeeds of petty theft and calls to break up late-night parties. So it was Sunday, and the Red Sox were playing, and the cops had gathered after the day shift for a beer or two.

"Dad." Ella turned to her father. "Sam Adams?"

As a police captain, Bryan O'Connor usually didn't come to Mo's—it wasn't a good idea to drink with his officers. But today they'd solved a big case. Today, Ella, Ricardo, and two other detectives had finally arrested Leo Esposito and the key players in the Boston Mafia.

"Sure, thanks, hon." He nodded to her and walked to a booth where two cops were already sitting. One of them moved over to give him space. "Excuse me while I go and brag about my daughter, who took down the Boston Mafia only two years into her detective career."

Ella chuckled. Warmth spread through her chest. She could always trust her dad to be proud of her. She knew that he'd never leave her. That he'd never betray her. She didn't know why her mom had left when she was young, and for years she'd wondered about her and even searched for her. But something in her understood even if people had to leave sometimes, there were those who would always stay. Like her dad, and her stepmother, Gloria, whom she'd started calling Mom about a year after she'd appeared in Dad's life, and who'd basically raised Ella.

She leaned on the bar and waved to her uncle Maurice, who winked at her as he drew the beer from the keg.

"Congratulations," he said. "I already heard."

She beamed. The pub smelled like beer and distantly like citrus wood polish, a scent she'd known all her life. "Couldn't have done it without Ricardo and Dad," she said. "And that tip Dad got about Mafia headquarters." He'd refused to share his source, even in the department, to protect the person who'd risked everything to come forward.

"Where is Ricardo?"

"Still at the station, but he'll join us soon."

Uncle Mo put two beers on the bar in front of him for someone who'd ordered before her, then turned to Ella. "Are you two still dating?"

She snorted. "No. It was one date, and it was so disastrous we still laugh about it. He just moved in with his girlfriend."

Mo leaned on the bar with both arms and chuckled. "Main thing is you are both okay. What can I get you, sweetheart?"

"Sam Adams for Dad, and um...you have any Guinness today?"

"Sure do. Coming up." He took a fresh glass and pulled the keg handle, and beer slid into the glass, dark and creamy. "Are you coming to visit again this weekend?"

She nodded. "As always. Ted already told me he drew some sort of Viking superhero...Ralf. He wants to show me."

"It's Rolf, actually," someone said to her left, and she turned her head.

Good God. He stood right next to her, smiling the most disarming, the most heartbreaking smile on the most handsome face she'd seen in some time. He was tall, a giant almost. Muscles bulged under his charcoal gray suit. She couldn't help noticing his broad shoulders, narrow waist, and strong pecs. Knotted Viking tattoos trailed along his neck and protruded from under the shirt cuff at his wrist. His long hair was partially captured in a man bun, and his green eyes watched her with something like amusement...and heat. God, so much heat. There was a birthmark on his temple, something like a heart. A short, sexy beard—more like long stubble —covered his square jaw, and full lips smiled crookedly at her.

Cocky.

The moment she inhaled his scent, she was lost. Something masculine, and earthy, and woody. His cologne, elegant and stylish and timeless, combined with the scent of his skin, and the mixture made her mouth water and sent her heart slamming against her chest. There was some sort of connection between them, an almost physical pull she had to actively resist.

She knew him from somewhere. He looked so familiar.

"Oh. Right. Rolf."

His suit was clearly very expensive and fit him perfectly, like a second skin. The watch on his wrist would probably cost her a year's salary. Detectives wore suits and watches, but not like these.

She forced her traitorous eyes to return to his face. "You don't look like someone who knows superheroes."

He arched one eyebrow. "You don't look like someone who belongs in a cop bar."

Heat rushed to her cheeks. "I'm not sure that's appropriate."

"Just an observation."

Okay. She lost all interest in him. Arrogant jerk, like all rich guys.

"Let me be quite direct, sir. Although it's unofficial, this *is* a cop bar, so...maybe you should find somewhere else to drink your...?"

He looked at Mo. "Can I please get a scotch?"

"Sure, it'll just be a moment." Mo pushed the glass of Guinness to Ella. "Don't worry, I'll take this to Bryan." He lifted the pint of Sam Adams and walked out from behind the bar.

She didn't want to stay and talk to this arrogant guy. And she wasn't going to. She picked up her Guinness and brushed past him. "Excuse me."

He caught her arm above her elbow and stopped her. The moment his skin touched hers through the thin material of her shirt, something happened.

It was like time slowed. Something surged through her, sweet and powerful, and electric. Golden, glowing threads were charging all around them. She couldn't breathe. No one and nothing else existed. Just him and her, and somehow, this was right.

Perhaps the most right thing in the world.

Still holding her arm, he said, "Tell me you felt it, too."

She couldn't move.

Her gaze dropped to his hand holding her. The cuff of his shirt had dragged up, revealing a tattoo on the inner side of his wrist, right above the radial artery.

A spindle.

A tingle ran down her spine. "Who are you?" she asked.

Dad appeared from behind the man, and he let her go, to her disappointment. "Ah, Ella, I see you already met our anonymous tipper. Now that the Mafia is behind bars, I don't have to protect his identity anymore. At least not from you."

Ella looked at the beautiful man with different eyes. He was the reason they had been able to get the final piece of proof and arrest the Mafia.

"I'm Channing Hakonson. And you are Ella…?" He waited as if for her to fill in the blank.

Ignoring the prompt, she said, "Oh, now I know where I know you from. You're the owner of the Port of Boston. The first completely green port in the world."

"I am."

So he wasn't a jerk after all. At least, not as big a one as she had thought he was. The man had created and funded an initiative to transform the shipping industry. He had dedicated one of the buildings in the port to research, hired two MIT scientists, and last month he had launched the first completely green transport ship. No carbon emissions. No oil or gas needed. But he was working with those who wanted to be part of the solution, helping them transition from oil and gas production to manufacturing the green fuel now in high demand.

He didn't look for easy ways, did he?

She liked him more and more.

Someone called for Captain O'Connor, and her dad got swallowed back into the crowd.

"I'm Ella O'Connor," she said. "Nice to meet you."

"Don't go. Let me buy you a drink," he said. "It's the least I can do to thank you for keeping Boston safe."

She chuckled. "You pay taxes, which pay my salary."

"Well…yes."

She gently removed her arm from his grasp and raised her Guinness. "I already have a drink."

"I'll buy you another one."

"Tell you what. Let me buy you a drink for once. I bet no one does that for you anymore."

He chuckled and stretched his arm towards the bar in an inviting gesture. "You have no idea how right you are."

She sat on a stool. "Remember that. It's quite likely you'll think that many, many times in the future."

He took a seat as well. "I like a strong woman who knows her mind. I've always thought the right woman is an axis. And the right man for her can't help but spin around it."

Something about those words echoed through her. Like she'd already heard this, already lived this moment.

It felt odd. Beautiful.

From the speakers, Disturbed started singing "The Sound of Silence," and the music pulled at her chest achingly.

She drank her beer. "I've often thought women are the ones who end up spinning around men. *I* certainly don't want a man who commands me and controls me. He'd get one in the nose."

He took her Guinness and drank. Something about it was so intimate, so seductive. Like he'd kissed the space where her lips touched. Like they'd already kissed, a long time ago.

"Keep it up," he said. "You sound like the perfect woman for me. If you're not careful, I may just marry you."

EPILOGUE

Three years later...

"CHANNING." Ella giggled. "Please stop."

He had no intention of stopping. He kissed her breast. "What you mean is keep going."

She giggled again, wriggling under his mouth. "Someone might come in."

He kissed her other breast, took the nipple in right through her maternity tunic. No bra. Her breasts were heavy and full and sensitive, and her nipples were so deliciously dark. "I don't care. I love you."

He looked up at her. The sun was shining right on her through the floor-to-ceiling window of their bedroom. Her skin was glowing, almost golden with the tan she'd gotten over the summer in their beach house in Gloucester, and with her pregnancy, she was ripe and beautiful and luscious. He wanted to fill this house with kids who had her eyes and her laugh.

She smiled. "And I love you. But we have guests, and they might come in."

He gently stroked her huge belly and planted a kiss. "I'll just close the door. And they're not guests. They're family."

They couldn't see her family from their bedroom, but the puffs of smoke that flew by their window came from the patio where Bryan was on grill duty making his delicious spareribs. Gloria was bustling about setting the outdoor table overlooking the sea, Ted was probably drawing in his new Rolf-themed sketchbook, working on his own comic. Ricardo and his wife were also there, as well as Uncle Mo and his family. Channing had invited his Boston University colleagues and Georgina and Munchie, the two scientists who now worked on green energy and recycling innovations. They were the ones who had made Boston the first green port in the world and had made sure their technologies were applicable in any port and shipbuilding industry. During the past three years, over two hundred ports around the world and over six hundred container ships had become green.

He pulled a quilt over the both of them, brought his hand down her belly and beneath her maternity pants, and gently stroked her where he knew she loved it the most. She opened up for him, warm and soft, and moved her pelvis to accommodate him, biting her lip and closing her eyes.

He murmured, "And Ciara needs to hurry up and be born. Isn't sex one of the best ways to start labor?"

Ciara was the name Ella had dreamed of one night. She'd woken up and told him she knew in her heart that was their little girl's name.

"It is..." she replied, her voice low and husky. "But we've been away from the guests for a while and—"

As though reading her thoughts, Ted opened the door and burst in.

Channing couldn't withdraw his hand in time and sat up, putting a cushion over his erection. Ella pulled her tunic down and sat up straighter in the bed, covering herself with the quilt. Her cheeks were flushed.

"Heeey, buddy," Channing said.

"Heeey, Ted…" Ella echoed and shoved Channing with her foot, as though to say, *I told you so.*

Ted stopped in the middle of the room and frowned, looking between them. "Why are you still here? You still don't feel well, Ella?"

He'd grown up a lot in the past three years and was a teen now. A talented artist, he drew every day, and art was his favorite subject at school.

"We're coming," Ella said.

"Gloria is about to bring out the cake."

"Okay," Channing said. He still couldn't stand up without showing a bulge between his legs. "We'll be right there, okay? We won't miss you blowing out your candles, buddy."

Ella squirmed and gasped, "Oh," and looked at her belly with wide eyes.

Ted didn't leave. Instead, he came towards them and sat right on the bed between them. "Did Ciara kick?" he asked.

Ella looked at Channing. "Yes, she did."

"Strong girl." Channing smiled.

"Uh-huh. So strong, my water just broke."

Happiness bloomed in his heart. He pushed the cushion away and took her by the hands. He looked into her eyes, sinking in their blue depths.

"I love you so much, Ella," he said and grinned.

"I love you, too." She grinned in return and shifted to get out of bed.

He had his home, his warm hearth, the woman who made

his life whole and his happiness complete. And he was ready for whatever happened next.

Because she was his axis. And he was a thread spinning around her.

And the threads of their lives were entangled, woven into a tapestry. It wasn't perfect. It wasn't always smooth.

But it sure took his breath away.

THANK you for reading AGE OF FIRE. I hope you loved Channing and Ella's story. This concludes the FATED series.

Other mysterious matchmakers help modern-day people find their soulmates in different eras, too. Keep reading:

- CALLED BY A HIGHLANDER series if you'd like to follow Amy back in time and into the strong arms of Highlander Craig,
- CALLED BY A VIKING series to travel back in time with Holly and into the arms of Viking jarl Einar (and find out more about Channing's backstory within the series).
- CALLED BY A PIRATE series to join Samantha on her journey through time and into the arms of Captain James "Prince" Barrow.

SIGN-UP FOR MY NEWSLETTER to find out when new books release, hear about exclusive giveaways, and take a sneak peek into my future books.

. . .

FANCY A HIGHLANDER?

She must return to her time. He keeps her heart captive. Can their love outlast the ages?

Read HIGHLANDER'S CAPTIVE now >

UP FOR A STRONG VIKING?

A captive time traveler. A Viking jarl on a mission. Will marriage be the price of her freedom?

Read VIKING'S DESIRE now >

READY FOR YOUR PIRATE?

A pirate desperate to lead an honest life. An executive who falls through time. One last chance to right the wrongs of the past.

Read PIRATES TREASURE now >

OR KEEP READING for an excerpt into the VIKING'S DESIRE, the first book of the CALLED BY A VIKING SERIES, where Channing's story has its beginning...

ORLANDO, Florida, May 3, 2019

"HOLLY, sweetheart, are you sure it's the wisest thing to go to Scotland two weeks before your big merger? You've been working so hard."

Holly clenched the handle of her suitcase harder as she walked through the departure area with her parents to drop off her luggage. Mom's brown eyes were worried—as always. The lines around her mouth deepened.

"Mom, really, everything is done. We're just waiting for the final paperwork to come through. In two weeks, we sign. I'll be back by then."

"A responsible person wouldn't leave right before closing an important deal," her mother said. "This is not how I raised you."

Holly suppressed a sigh and stood at the end of the baggage drop line. Mom meant well. It was just hard to see that sometimes behind the criticizing comments. Holly turned and faced her parents. They were so different from her—her mom, a petite, sweet-looking woman with a mane of curly gray hair; her dad, tall, handsome, and broad-shouldered; a true army man.

Of course, Holly didn't look like either of them.

"Mom, I haven't taken a vacation in three years. The genealogy researcher in Inverness has a very long waiting list, and her next opening is in two years. It's a rare chance to find out about my roots."

"But why do you need to find out about *them* when you have us?" Mom said. "Haven't we given you everything?"

Dad hugged her. "Gemma, let her do it. You don't know what it's like..."

Holly flashed a grateful smile at her dad. He was a man of few words, but when he said them, they were the right ones. Holly was more like him than her mom, who had a lot to say on many subjects.

The line moved and Holly went to check in her luggage and get her boarding pass. Once she was done, she returned to her parents.

"Should we go for a coffee?" Mom asked.

Holly flashed a polite smile. "Mom, I better get going. I still need to send a couple of emails before the flight."

Her mom sighed. "I suppose."

The three of them proceeded towards the security check.

"I just keep thinking I forgot to tell you something," Mom said. "I have this uneasiness in my heart about your trip. As if I'm seeing you for the last t—"

She cut herself off, tears gathering in her eyes. Holly squeezed her mom's shoulder.

"Everything will be fine, Mom."

Holly's dad hugged her mom. "Gemma, she's traveled the world. It's Scotland, not Siberia. And she's a grown, successful woman."

Mom cocked her head. "A successful woman doesn't date a sperm bank."

Here we go.

"This is why you wanted to go for a coffee, Mom? To berate me about my wish to have children?"

"It's unnatural, honey. You need a husband first."

"And what if I don't have one, huh, Mom? What if men literally run in the other direction after they get to know the real me? Should that stop me? Nowadays, a woman doesn't need a man to raise—"

"Those men are idiots. And yes, a woman does need a partner to raise a child. How many times have you tried? Five? Six?"

Holly's eyes watered. Why was it that people closest to her had the capacity to hurt her the most?

"Last month was seven," Holly said. "You're right. It's probably not meant to be. Something must be wrong with me."

Mom grimaced and hugged Holly with one arm. "I know very well how it is, dear. God never gave me the chance to give birth, but he gave me you. In preparation for when the right man comes, maybe you need to try eating healthier or cut out coffee. You know I raised you to achieve things despite your flaws."

"I guess this flaw is too big to be overcome," Holly said, wiping her eyes and leaving black smudges of mascara on the backs of her hands and undoubtedly on her face.

From the corner of Holly's eye, she saw a flash of movement. She glanced to her left and noticed a big tall man with a cart full of suitcases marching towards them at full speed. He was looking at his phone.

Holly barely managed to jerk her mother out of his path, steadying her to keep her from falling.

"Sir, please watch where you're going," Holly said.

The man glanced over his phone, raised his hand without stopping. "Sorry, sorry, late for my flight." He continued marching, his eyes glued to his phone.

"Thank you, sweetheart," Mom said. "You've always protected me, ever since you were little—even from spiders."

Holly chuckled. Her mom could seem harsh at times, but she was terrified of spiders.

They stopped at the end of the line to the security check, which, thankfully, had only three people waiting.

"Behave well, Holly." Mom straightened Holly's blouse as though before her first day at school. "Don't drink too much whiskey, don't sleep around, and don't forget us."

Holly gasped and shook her head. "Mom, I can't believe you just said that. I do not sleep around!"

"Well, you have no man in your life, and those Highlanders..." She threw a glance at Dad as she trailed off.

"Stop talking to me like I'm a child," Holly said. "I'm thirty-five for God's sake. You didn't even have to bring me to the airport—I have a car!"

"Ah, nonsense. Someone had to make sure you didn't forget your luggage somewhere."

Holly took a deep breath, trying to calm her nerves. *She means well,* she told herself. *She means well. She just doesn't know how to show it.*

"Mom, I run a billion-dollar company. I don't tend to forget much."

Mom smiled and cupped her face. "You're right, dear. Please call us when you land."

She hugged Holly. Dad smiled apologetically and hugged her, too. He kissed the crown of her head and whispered, "We love you, hon."

Holly waved to them and joined the line at the security check, the tension in her shoulders finally releasing. Once she had a few days away from home and her parents, she hoped she would be able to forget that something was clearly wrong with her. She would read the book about medieval Scotland and Vikings and drink as much coffee as she wanted on the plane.

And maybe, just maybe, she'd find out where she really came from and why her real parents had rejected her.

NEAR THE VILLAGE OF TONGUE, Sutherland, Northern Scotland, May 5, 2019

TOGETHER WITH MS. VERDANDI, the genealogy researcher from Inverness, Holly walked towards the edge of the bare green coast that spread to the left and right. At the edge of the cliffs in front of them, in the middle of the green grass, stood a giant ash tree. Holly felt a strange pull towards the tree, as though she needed to touch it. Maybe it was because there were no other trees in sight for miles and miles.

Holly sped up, cautious not to overwhelm the old lady,

whose lilac suit was a strange contrast with the wildness of the sight. But she didn't need to worry. Ms. Verdandi looked eighty but seemed to have more agility and strength than Holly.

Behind the tree and the cliffs was the North Sea, dark blue now in the sunlight. A breeze brought the scents of sea, sun, and warm rocks, and Holly inhaled it deeply, a smile spreading on her face. The air here was very different from Orlando. It felt cool and fresh, and even the scent felt *green*. It was the scent of freedom.

"So, this is where it happened?" Holly said when they stood by the tree. "Vikings kidnapped my great-great-great..." Holly laughed. "I don't even know how many 'greats' I need to add to 'grandmother.'"

Ms. Verdandi echoed her laugh.

"Yes, they did," she said in her strange accent that was definitely not Scottish. "Northern Scotland has always had a deep connection with the Vikings." Her eyes twinkled mischievously.

"Near the ash tree, there was a big village that went from here down to the beach."

Ms. Verdandi gestured to the left, where the green surface of the cliff descended to a small, secluded white-sand beach.

"Later, Clan MacKay would rule here. Your ancestor who was kidnapped, she would be a MacKay. You have both Scottish and Norse blood, dear," she said.

Holly raised her brows. "Well, yes, that's what the DNA ancestry test said."

The woman smiled. "I did not need a DNA test to tell you that. Norse heritage is written all over you. That steel in your eyes. The strength. The honesty. The honor. The endurance and commitment you have to protect your loved ones no matter what."

A small shiver ran through Holly's skin. The words rang

true and reverberated within her deeply. "You can tell all of that by just looking at me?"

The edges of the woman's eyes creased in many small wrinkles. "You just need to know where to look. I also see that you have magic in your blood. You have quite a few *völvas* and witches in your line."

Holly laughed. "Right. And the sky turned red and there were dragons breathing fire. Oh, you do not seriously believe that, do you?"

The woman arched one eyebrow and said, "Look at the tree. What do you see?"

Holly studied the tree. It was massive, tall, and thick, with big roots gripping the rocky soil. How had it even managed to grow on these cliffs? Bare branches rustled in the wind.

Bare tree. Bare land. Barren like Holly.

Tears pricked her eyes. God, why was it so important to her? She didn't even have a man in her life.

But she'd always wanted a child of her own. Flesh and blood. Although she loved her parents, maybe that feeling of being broken, being faulty, was because she had been rejected by her biological mother.

She looked at the trunk and frowned. Something was carved on it—an intricate, ornate, interwoven pattern. Something Celtic or Viking. How had she not noticed this before? Holly looked closer. Something long and sharp at the edges.

A spindle.

Holly glanced for a moment at Ms. Verdandi, puzzled. "What does it mean?"

"Just look," she said, a sly smile spreading her lips.

Holly looked again and gasped. Instead of the wooden spindle on the trunk, it was golden, and the patterns weren't carved anymore but engraved. She stepped closer and brushed her index finger along the length of the spindle. It was smooth, and it buzzed slightly. Holly pulled her hand away.

"Neat trick," she said with a nervous laugh. "How did you do it?"

"Ah, you'll learn. You were looking for a tree, dear? You found it."

"I wasn't looking for a tree. I was looking for information about my ancestors."

"A genealogical tree, dear."

Holly smiled. "Ah. Well, yes. If you put it that way."

"Your roots lie with the Vikings...but also your future."

"Excuse me?"

"Look at the spindle, Holly." As if hypnotized, Holly looked. "There's a man who needs you back in the ninth century. He will help you find answers to all your questions, and his love will heal the cracks in your heart."

The spindle began to move towards the surface of the tree, as though pushed from within the trunk. Holly gasped, and as the spindle popped out of the surface completely, she automatically reached out her hand to catch the falling object.

The old lady's words reverberated through her whole body: "There is a man who needs you back in the ninth century. Your roots lie with the Vikings...but also your future."

Something invisible grabbed Holly's hand and pulled, something warm and hard and woody. Holly screamed and began struggling as she was pulled into the tree. She dug her heels into the ground, but the force was too strong. Then the trunk closed around her.

And darkness enveloped her.

Daylight blinded her as she was thrown forward with a violent jerk, as though someone had pushed her from behind. She fell to the ground, scratching the skin of her palms.

Screams rang in the air. The acrid smell of smoke filled her nostrils. Fear kicked her in the stomach. Adrenaline gathered her nerves like hair and pulled at them. She was still on what looked like the same Scottish coast and cliffs, except there was no Ms. Verdandi and no tree. About ten feet from her stood round stone houses with thatched cone-shaped roofs—and they were burning. Behind them, there was a medieval village on the green slope of the cliff leading towards the white-sand beach.

And among the houses, people dressed in medieval clothes fought. Some had axes and even swords, others only sticks and pitchforks.

But they not only fought, they also killed. They hauled people towards the beach. Down there, men carried sacks, furs, and even people towards three ships that looked Viking.

What the hell was this? The old woman had said Holly would travel to the ninth century.

The ninth century?!

But Holly could not actually travel in time, could she? This was ridiculous. This must be some hallucination or trick, or a prank. Maybe some sort of movie set.

But the air was thick with the iron tang of blood, and the weapons were metal, not plastic or rubber, because they cut flesh and spilled blood. There were no cameras, no directors, and no one telling the actors to run or stab or do any of that.

Holly's throat clenched, and she jumped to her feet, obeying the instinct to run and hide.

Frantically, she searched for an escape, for some way—

A man with a bloody ax and a predatory look stared right at her. The ground sank under her feet. He was tall and broad, his shoulders like boulders.

As he walked towards her, a single braid that came from the middle of his shaven head swung. His beard couldn't hide a sly smile.

Holly turned and ran. Away from the village, back towards

the small packed-dirt road where Ms. Verdandi had parked the car. If only she could get to the car...

She ran and ran, wind whistling in her ears, but he was closing in on her. And the road was nowhere to be seen. Nor was the car.

He grabbed her, and she stumbled and fell. Then he got on top of her. The impact kicked the air out of her. Pain radiated from the center of her stomach, and she choked under his weight. He turned her to face him, his pale-blue eyes piercing her. The ornate dragon tattoos on his shaven skull glistened in the dull light.

"And who do we have here?" he whispered, putting the bloody handle of his ax to her throat. His beard tickled her chin. "A witch. Are you a völva? I saw you appear out of thin air. Tell me."

She finally gasped in a breath. He was speaking some foreign language, her mind registered distantly. Holly had only learned Spanish in high school, and this was not Spanish. How was it possible that she understood him?

"No matter. You shall tell me on the way to the Orkneys."

He stood and picked her up as though she didn't weigh anything, putting her over his shoulder.

"Let me go!" Holly yelled. She kicked and drummed her fists against his back. But it was as though the giant didn't feel a thing. He just spanked her on her behind, so hard her whole body hurt.

"Shut up, witch. I thought Odin had forgotten Thorir Tree-beard, but he sent me a witch. Odin loves men who dare destiny. And what better way to do that than sacrifice a völva to the one-eyed god?"

KEEP READING VIKING'S DESIRE.

ALSO BY MARIAH STONE

Mariah's Time travel Romance Series

- CALLED BY A HIGHLANDER
- CALLED BY A VIKING
- CALLED BY A PIRATE
- FATED

Mariah's Regency Romance Series

- DUKES AND SECRETS

View all of Mariah's Books in Reading Order

Scan the QR code for the complete list of Mariah's ebooks, paperbacks, and audiobooks in reading order.

GET A FREE MARIAH STONE BOOK!

Join Mariah's mailing list to be the first to know of new releases, free books, special prices, and other author giveaways.

freehistoricalromancebooks.com

ENJOY THE BOOK? YOU CAN MAKE A DIFFERENCE!

Please, leave your honest review for the book.
As much as I'd love to, I don't have financial capacity like New York publishers to run ads in the newspaper or put posters in subway.

But I have something much, much more powerful!

Committed and loyal readers

If you enjoyed the book, I'd be so grateful if you could spend five minutes leaving a review on the book's Amazon page.

Thank you very much!

ABOUT MARIAH STONE

Mariah Stone is a bestselling author of time travel romance novels, including her popular Called by a Highlander series and her hot Viking, Pirate, and Regency novels. With nearly one million books sold, Mariah writes about strong modern-day women falling in love with their soulmates across time. Her books are available worldwide in multiple languages in e-book, print, and audio.

Subscribe to Mariah's newsletter for a free time travel romance book today at mariahstone.com/signup/!

facebook.com/mariahstoneauthor

instagram.com/mariahstoneauthor

bookbub.com/authors/mariah-stone

pinterest.com/mariahstoneauthor

amazon.com/Mariah-Stone/e/B07JVW28PJ